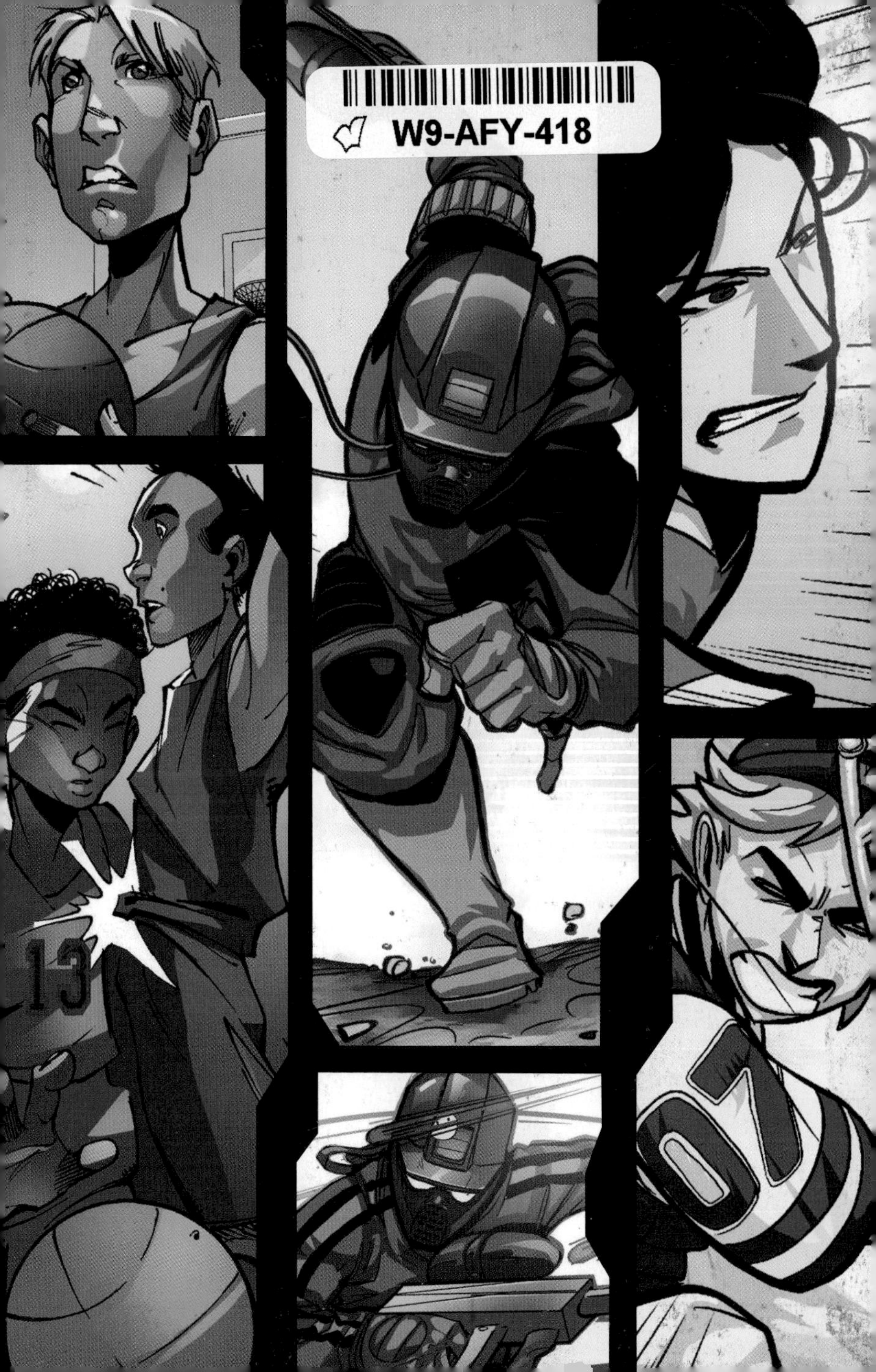

UP NEXT ›››

on Sports Illustrated KIDS

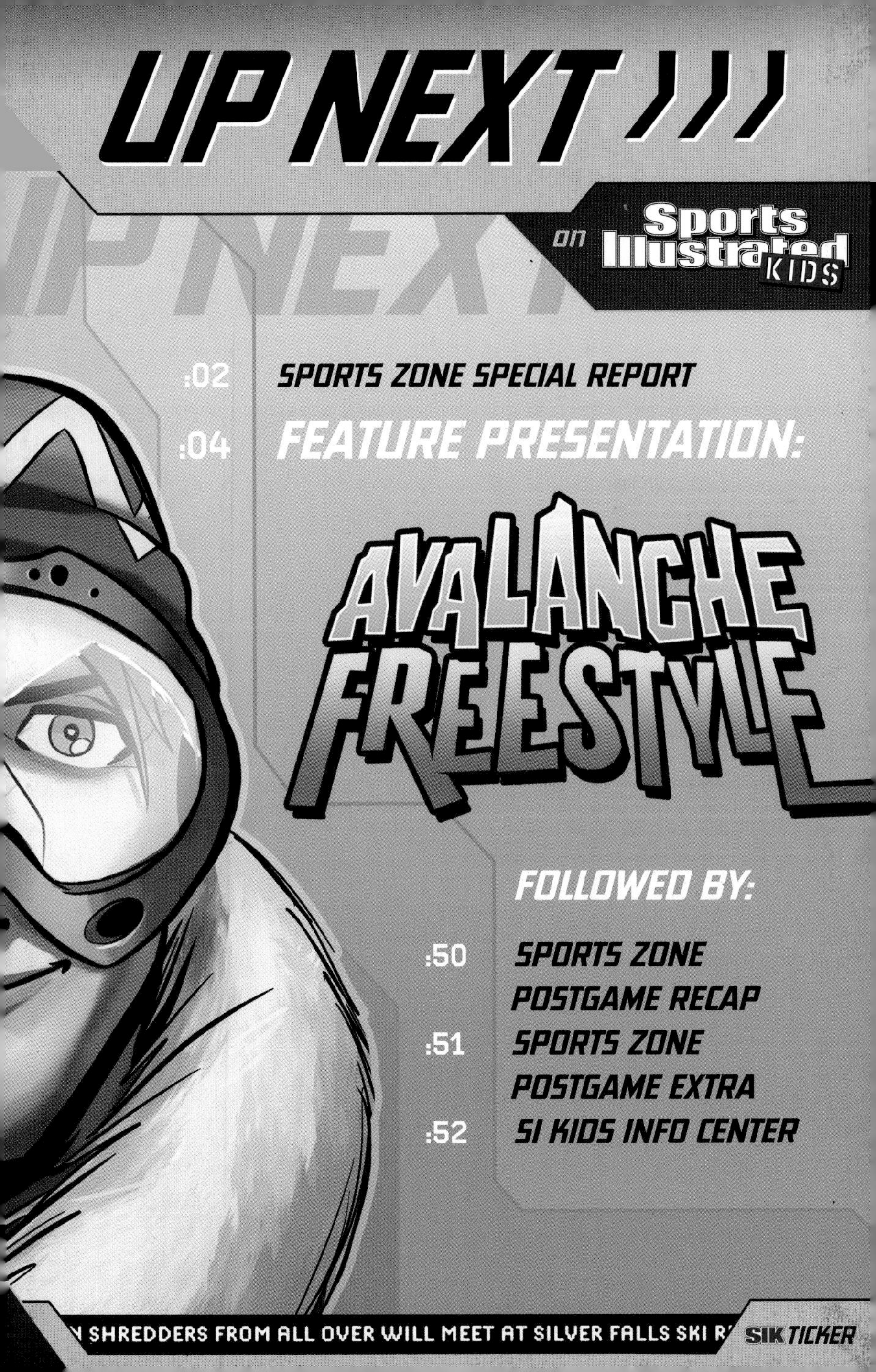

:02 SPORTS ZONE SPECIAL REPORT

:04 FEATURE PRESENTATION:

AVALANCHE FREESTYLE

FOLLOWED BY:

:50 SPORTS ZONE POSTGAME RECAP

:51 SPORTS ZONE POSTGAME EXTRA

:52 SI KIDS INFO CENTER

N SHREDDERS FROM ALL OVER WILL MEET AT SILVER FALLS SKI R

SIK TICKER

PORTS ZONE

CIAL REPORT

0
ING

TOP-RANKED TONY JAY IS EARLY FAVORITE TO WIN SILVER FALLS TOURNAMENT

AL
AURORA

TONY JAY

STATS:
AGE: 15
EVENT: FREESTYLE

BIO: Tony's father, Calvin Jay, is the owner of Silver Falls Ski Resort. Calvin bought his son the best gear that money can buy, and Tony's skills are second to none. In fact, the only shredder who has a shot at taking down Tony is Jack Hewlitt. There's just one problem — poor Jack can't afford to enter the competition, meaning that Tony will likely take home first place — and the fabled Aurora-X snowboard!

ports
strated
KIDS

UP NEXT: AVALANCHE FREESTYLE

JACK HEWLITT

AGE: 15
EVENT: FREESTYLE

BIO: Jack is a gifted shredder despite having to use a shabby board and well-worn bindings. Although his equipment is nowhere near top-notch, his skills are second to none, and he'll give Tony Jay a run for his money if he can find a way to enter the tournament...

BLZ vs BHS
3·1
TGR vs ROR
33·32
EAG vs BAN
14·7
SPA vs WLD
4·3
BAN vs ROR
21·15
ROR vs LIG
4·3
BLZ vs BHS
3·1

DWAYNE KENT

AGE: 15
BIO: Dwayne is one of Tony Jay's many friends. Like Janice and Kevin, Dwayne is almost always hanging out at the Jay family's mansion.

DWAYNE

CALVIN JAY

AGE: 43
BIO: Tony's father is a wealthy businessman who made a fortune in the music business. Now, he owns and runs the Silver Falls Ski Resort.

CALVIN

MARC HEWLITT

AGE: 47
BIO: Jack's father is a maintenance worker at Silver Falls Ski Resort. He does not make much money, but he loves his job — and his son.

MARC

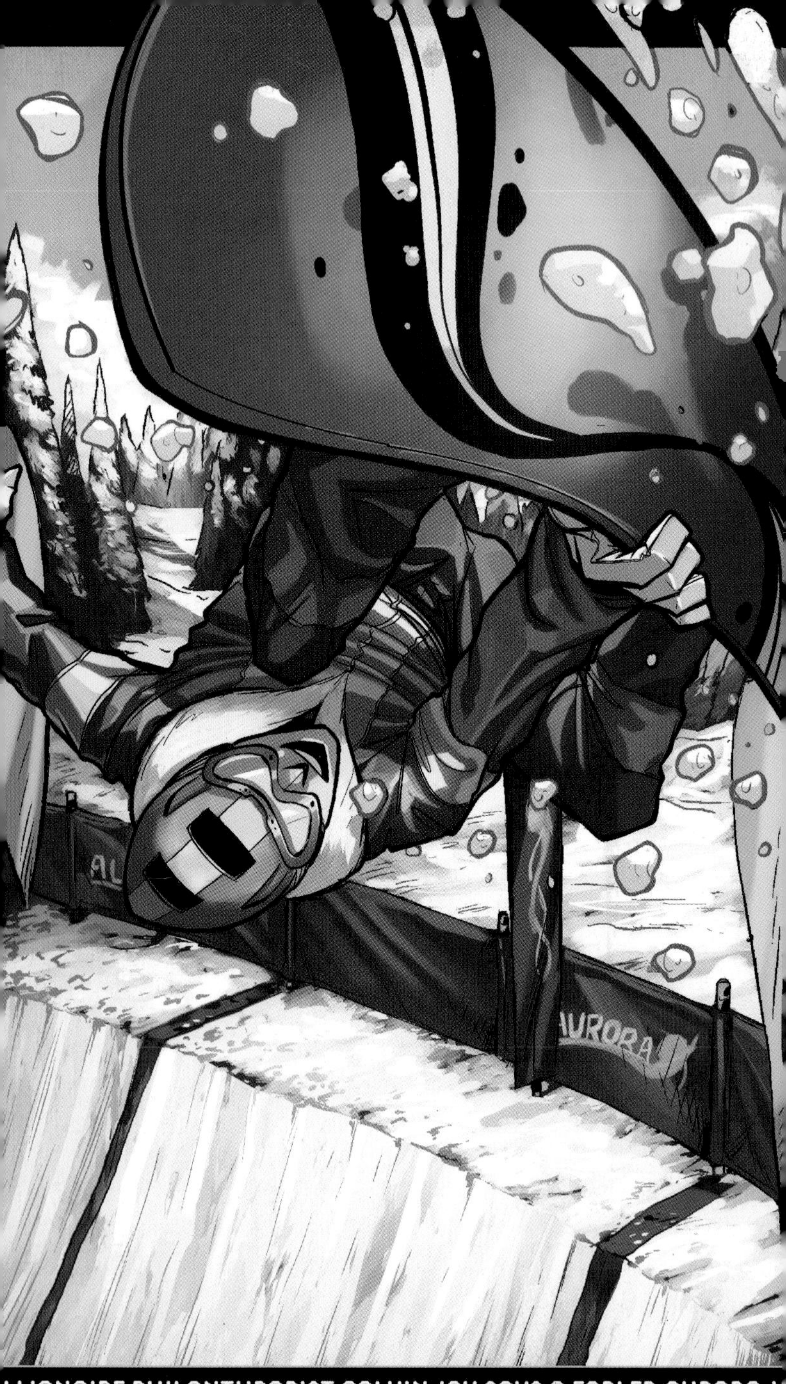
AURORA

LLIONAIRE PHILANTHROPIST CALVIN JAY SAYS A FABLED AURORA-X

Sports Illustrated KIDS

PRESENTS

A PRODUCTION OF

STONE ARCH BOOKS
a capstone imprint

written by Scott Ciencin
illustrated by Aburtov
inked by Andres Esparza
colored by Fares Maese

designed and directed by Bob Lentz
edited by Sean Tulien
creative direction by Heather Kindseth
editorial direction by Michael Dahl

Sports Illustrated KIDS *Avalanche Freestyle* is published by Stone Arch Books,
1710 Roe Crest Drive, North Mankato, Minnesota 56003.
www.capstonepub.com

Summary: Rich kid Tony Jay is a sure bet to win the Silver Falls
snowboarding tournament, but his biggest competition, Jack Hewlitt, can't
afford to enter. Tony may be spoiled, but he knows that victory means
nothing if you don't beat the best. So, he agrees to hold a one-on-one
freestyle contest with Jack atop the Silver Falls Mountains. But just when
things start to heat up, a massive avalanche threatens to put both boys on
ice, turning their friendly competition into a race for their lives.

Cataloging-in-Publication Data is available at the Library of Congress
website.

ISBN: 978-1-4342-2009-7 (library binding)
ISBN: 978-1-4342-2783-6 (paperback)
ISBN: 978-1-4342-4938-8 (e-book)

Printed in the United States of America.
052016   009789R

RD WILL GO TO THE WINNER OF HIS SNOWBOARDING TOURNAMEN **SIK** *TICKER*

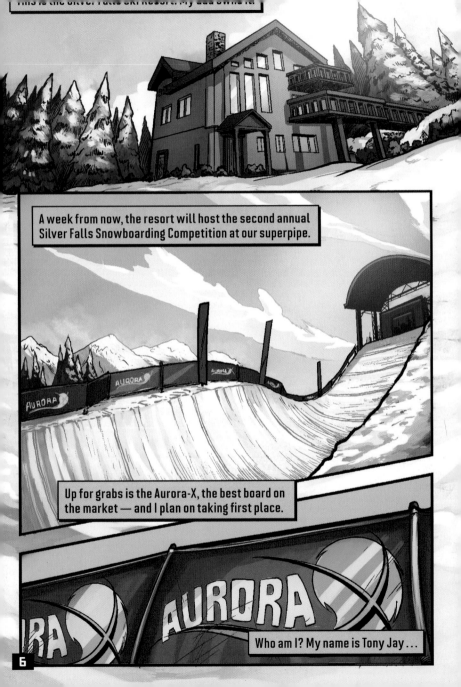

This is the Silver Falls Ski Resort. My dad owns it.

A week from now, the resort will host the second annual Silver Falls Snowboarding Competition at our superpipe.

Up for grabs is the Aurora-X, the best board on the market — and I plan on taking first place.

Who am I? My name is Tony Jay ...

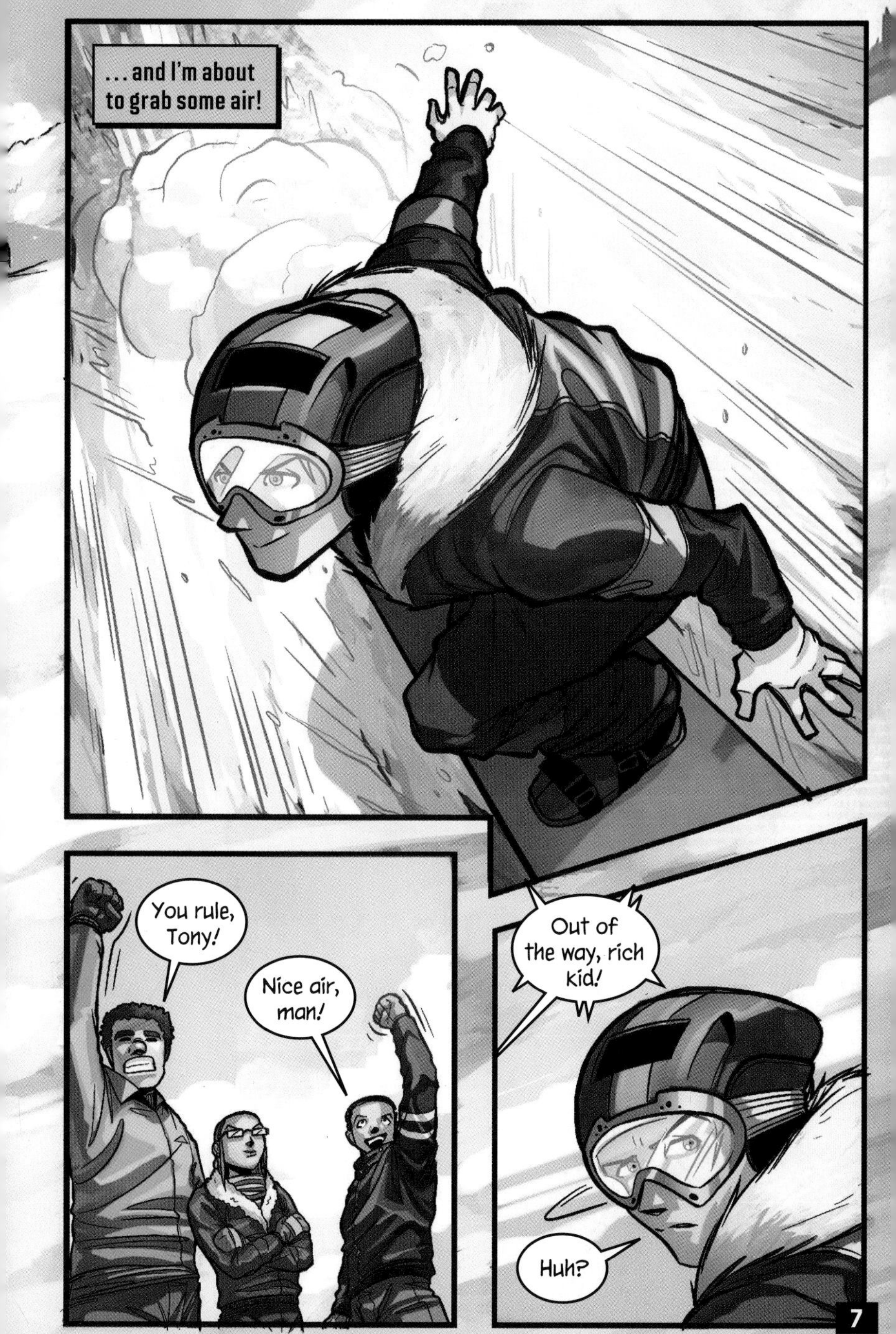

... and I'm about to grab some air!
You rule, Tony!
Nice air, man!
Out of the way, rich kid!
Huh?

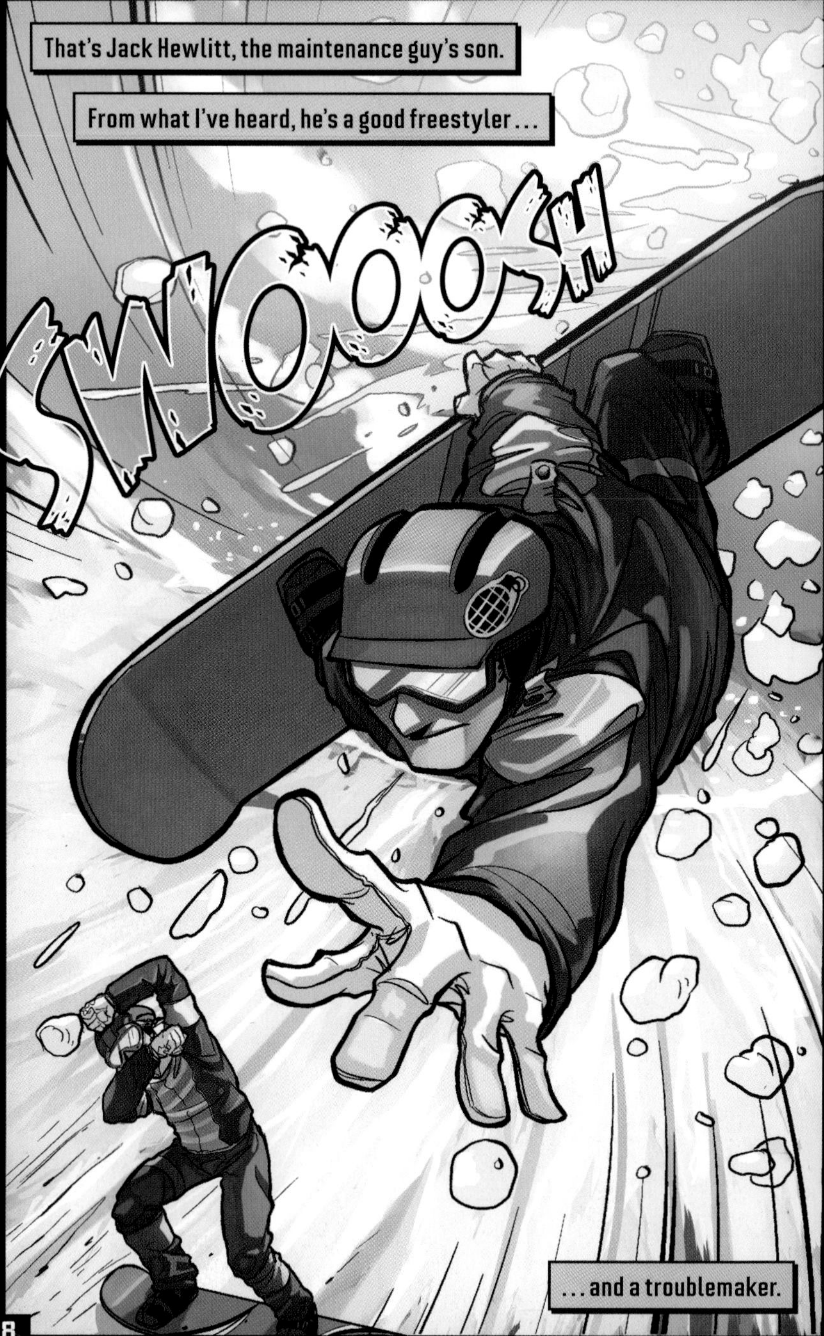
That's Jack Hewlitt, the maintenance guy's son.
From what I've heard, he's a good freestyler . . .
SWOOOSH
. . . and a troublemaker.

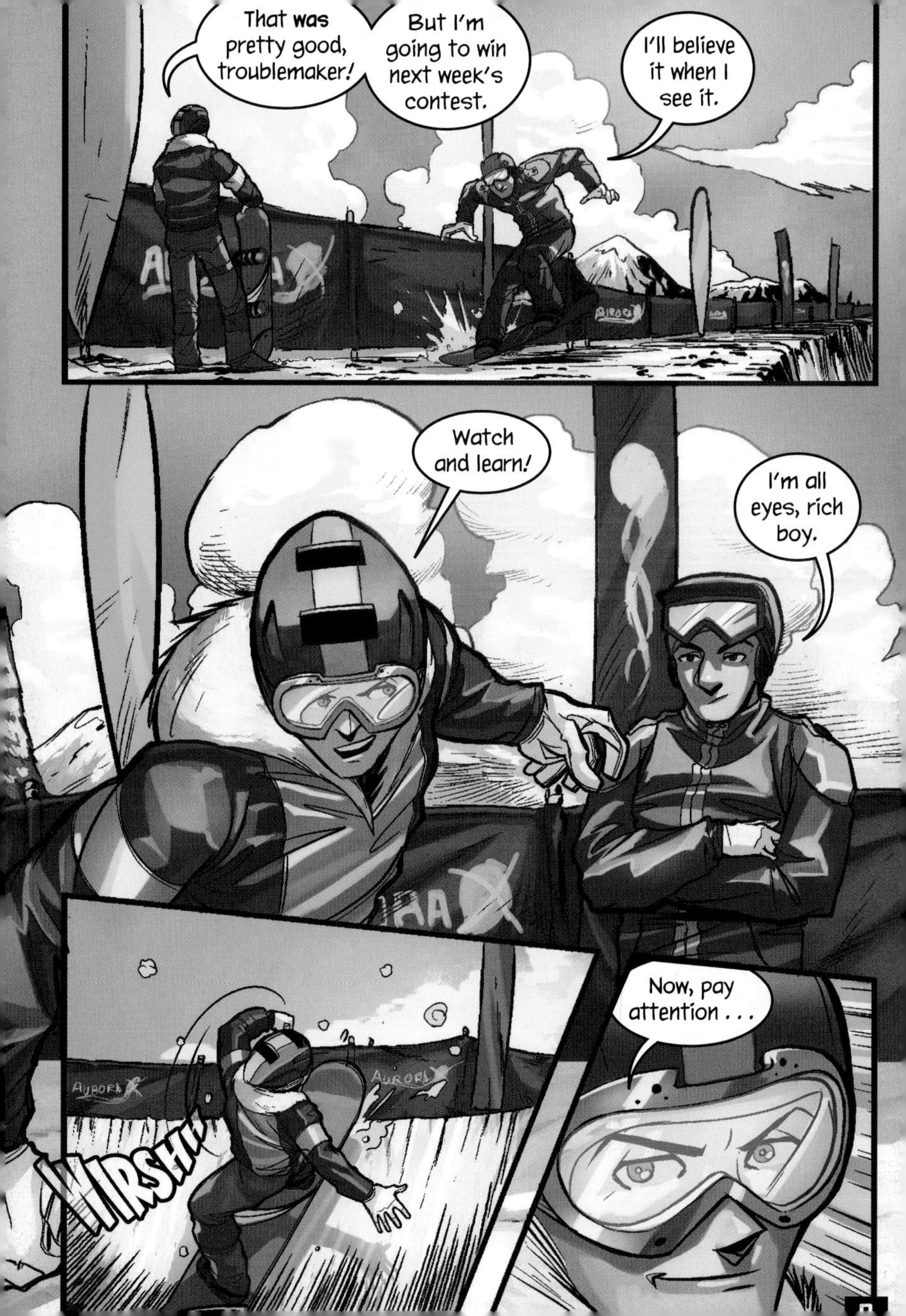
That was pretty good, troublemaker!
But I'm going to win next week's contest.
I'll believe it when I see it.
Watch and learn!
I'm all eyes, rich boy.
WIRSHH
Now, pay attention . . .

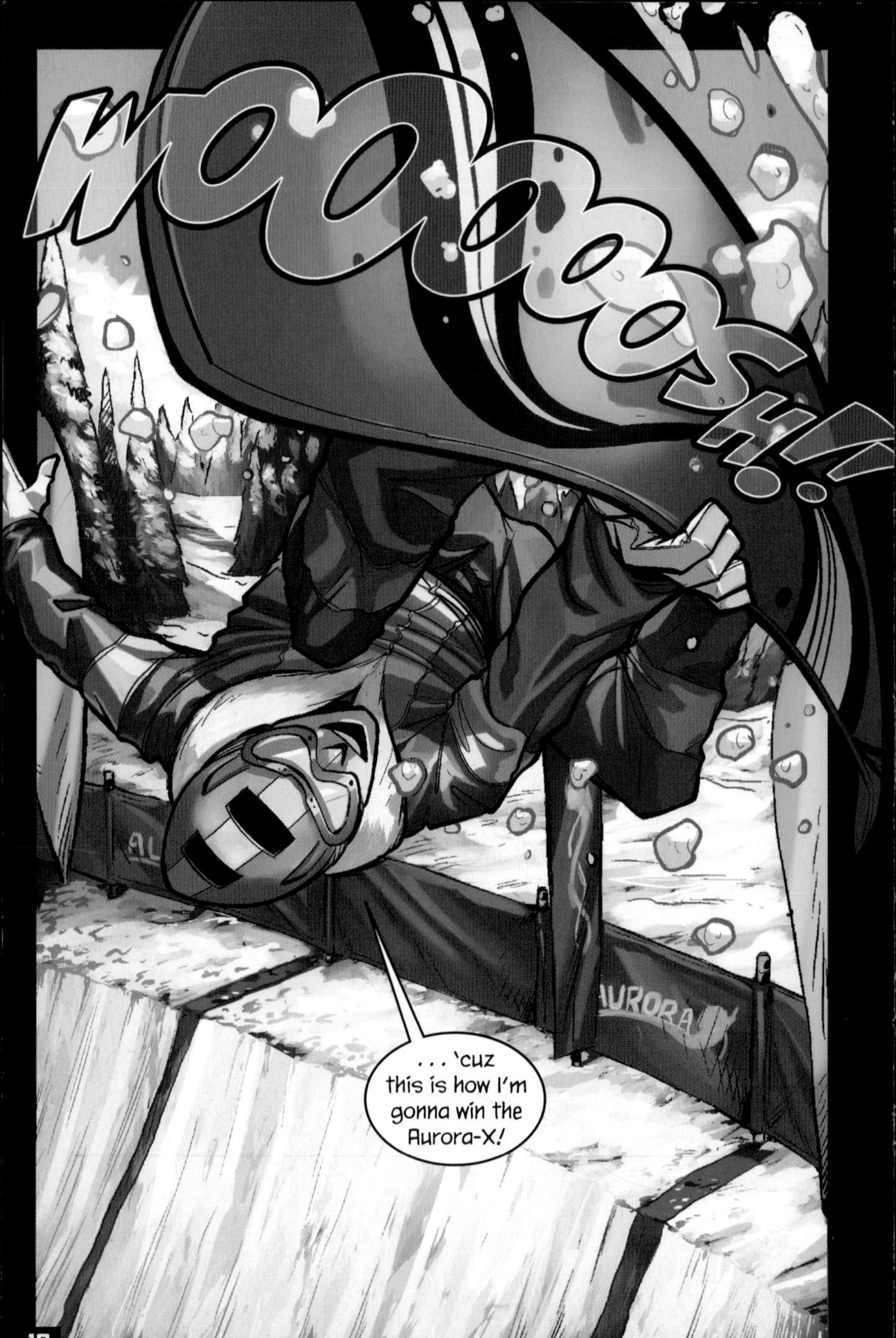
WOOOOOSH!!
. . . 'cuz this is how I'm gonna win the Aurora-X!

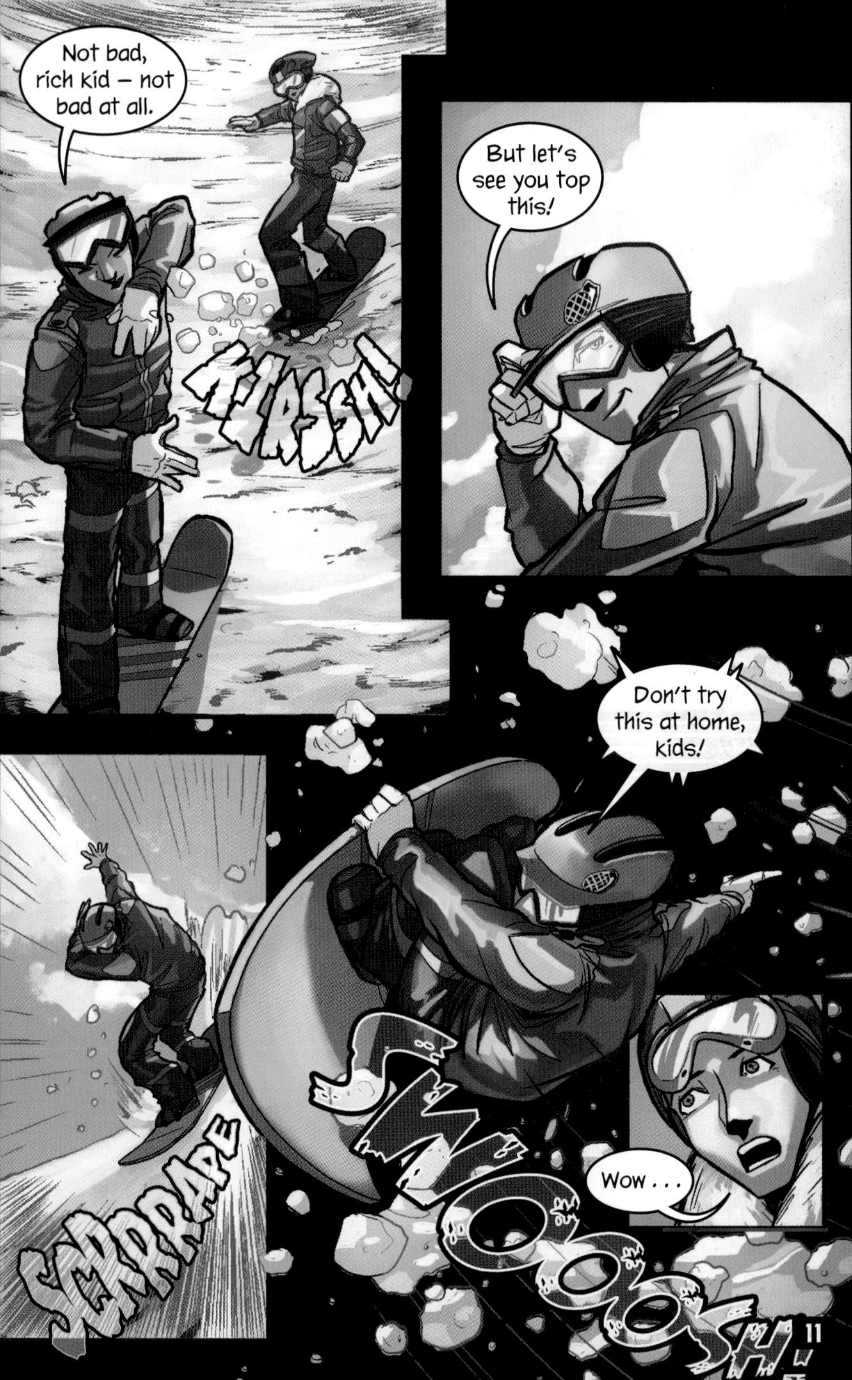
Not bad, rich kid — not bad at all.
But let's see you top this!
Don't try this at home, kids!
Wow . . .

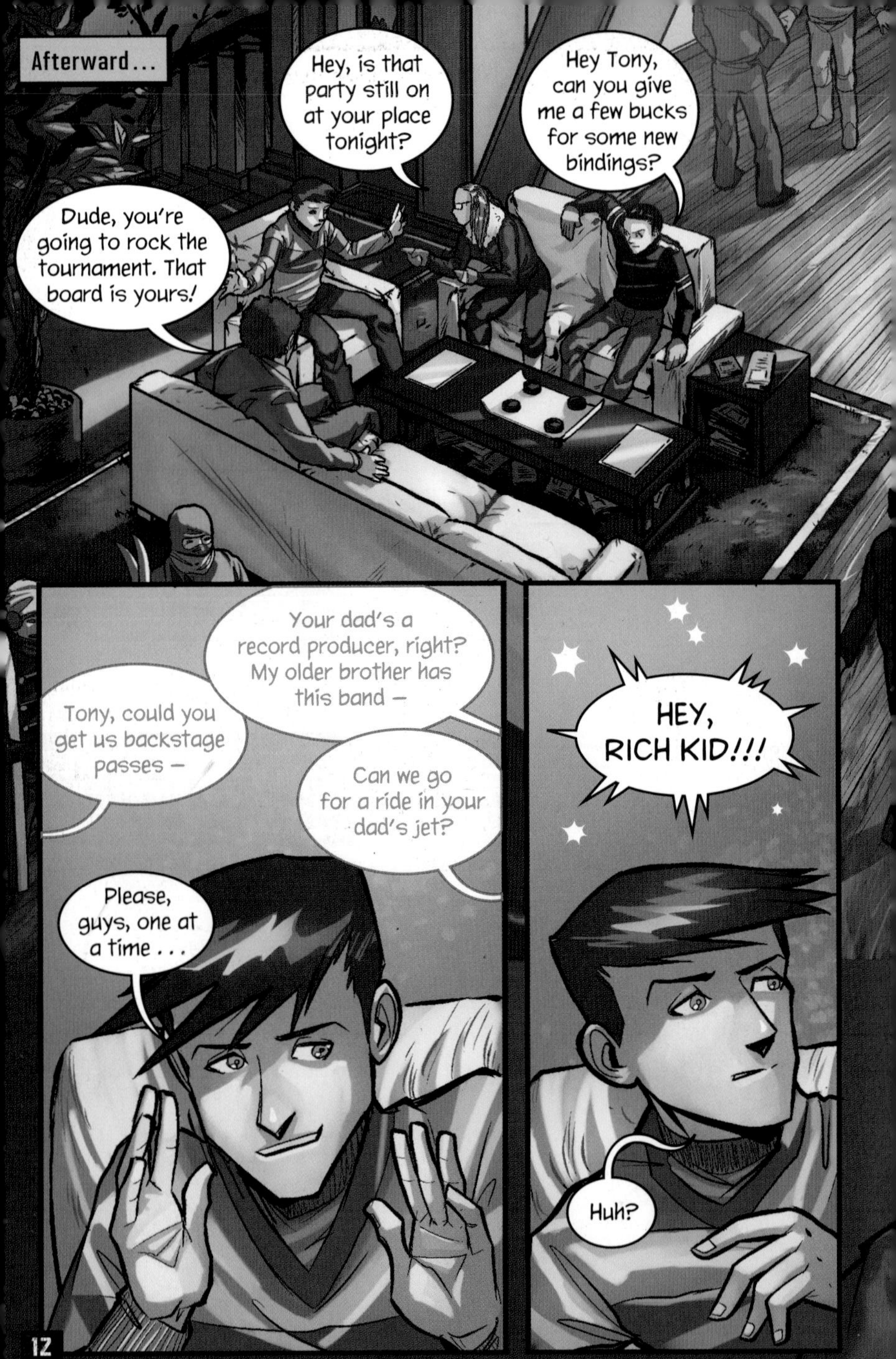
Afterward...
Hey, is that party still on at your place tonight?
Hey Tony, can you give me a few bucks for some new bindings?
Dude, you're going to rock the tournament. That board is yours!
Your dad's a record producer, right? My older brother has this band –
Tony, could you get us backstage passes –
Can we go for a ride in your dad's jet?
Please, guys, one at a time . . .
HEY, RICH KID!!!
Huh?

It's a shame that board's going to the best shredder who can **afford** to enter the competition . . .
. . . And not the best shredder at Silver Falls.
You're right. A victory wouldn't matter if I didn't beat the best.
So what do you have in mind, Jack?

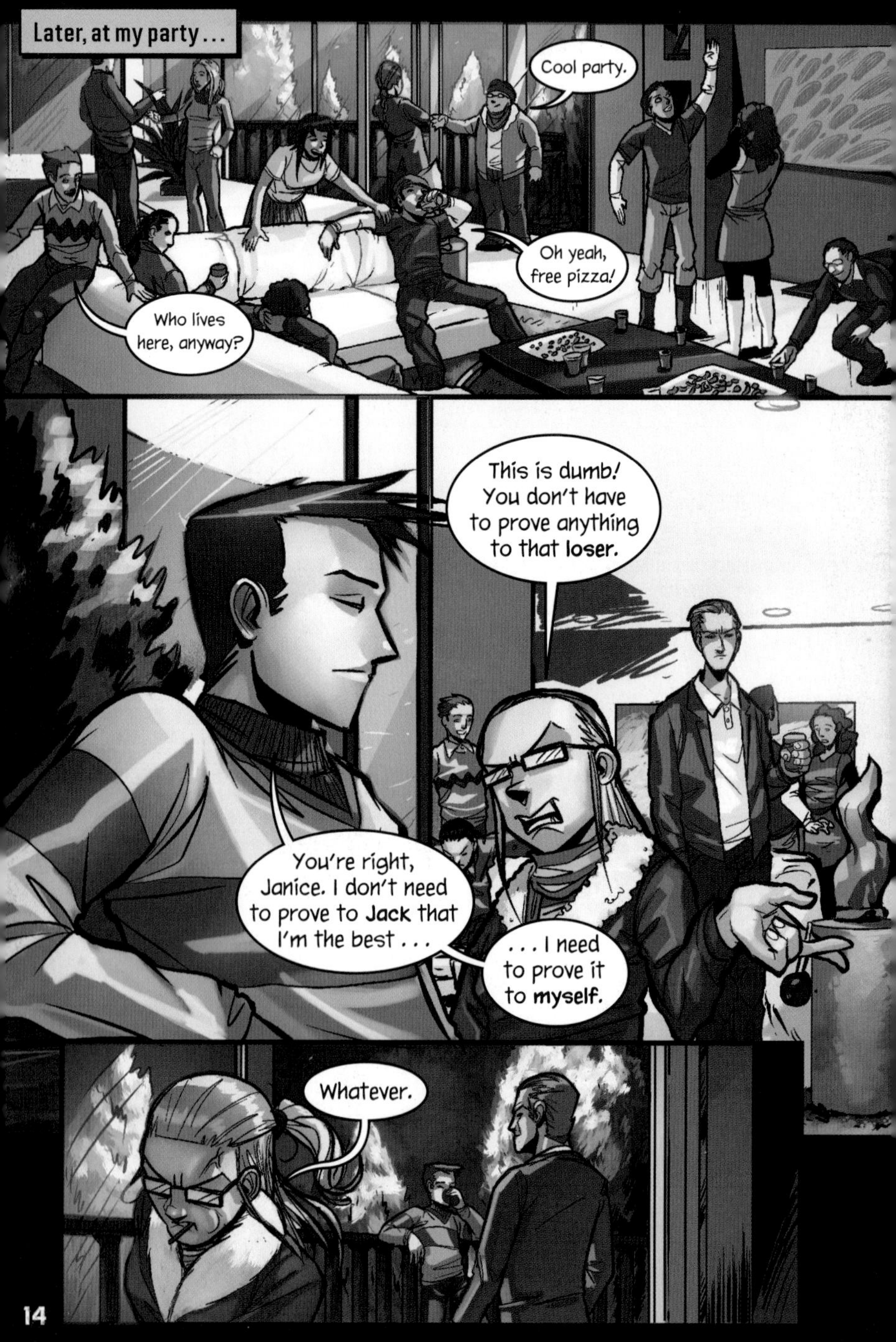
Later, at my party . . .
Cool party.
Oh yeah, free pizza!
Who lives here, anyway?
This is dumb! You don't have to prove anything to that loser.
You're right, Janice. I don't need to prove to Jack that I'm the best . . .
. . . I need to prove it to myself.
Whatever.

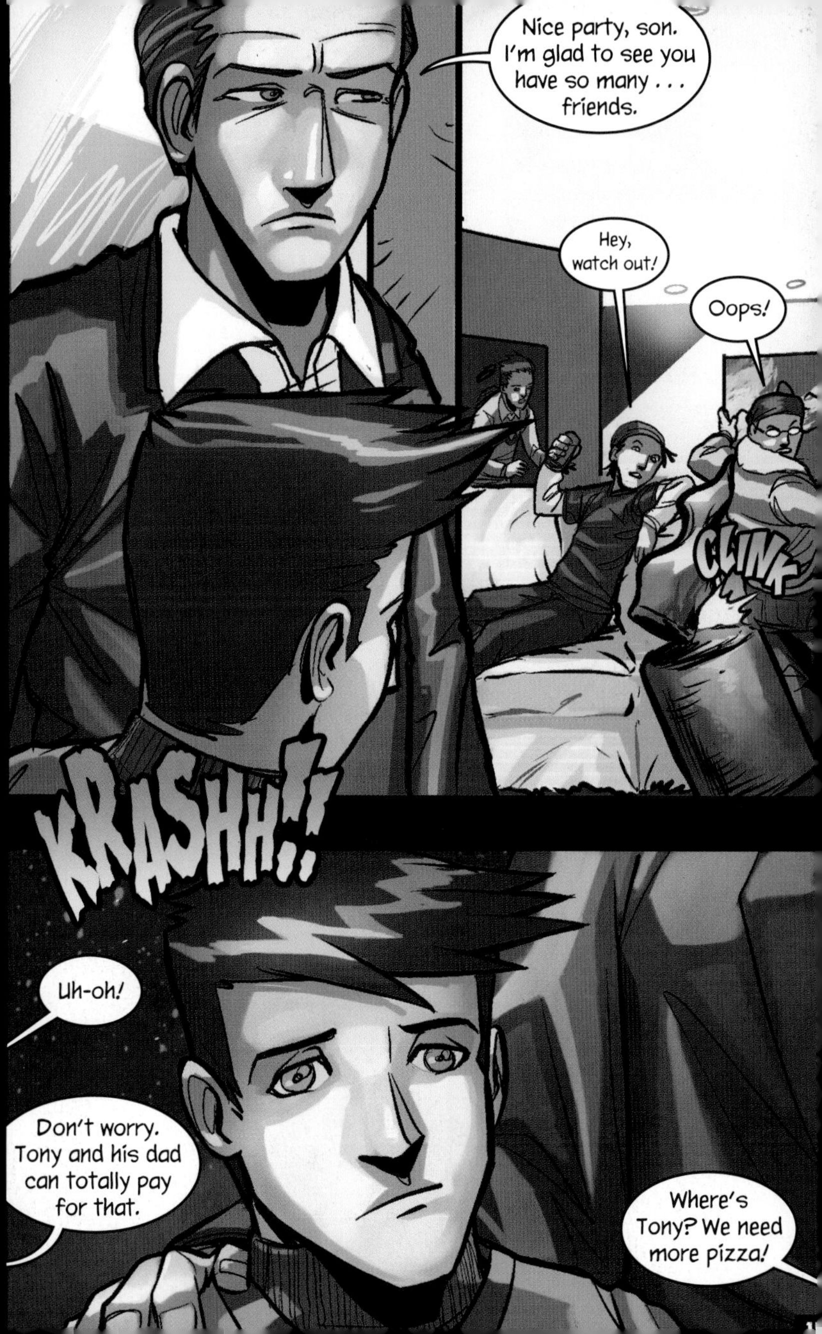
Nice party, son. I'm glad to see you have so many . . . friends.
Hey, watch out!
Oops!
CLINK
KRASHH!!
Uh-oh!
Don't worry. Tony and his dad can totally pay for that.
Where's Tony? We need more pizza!

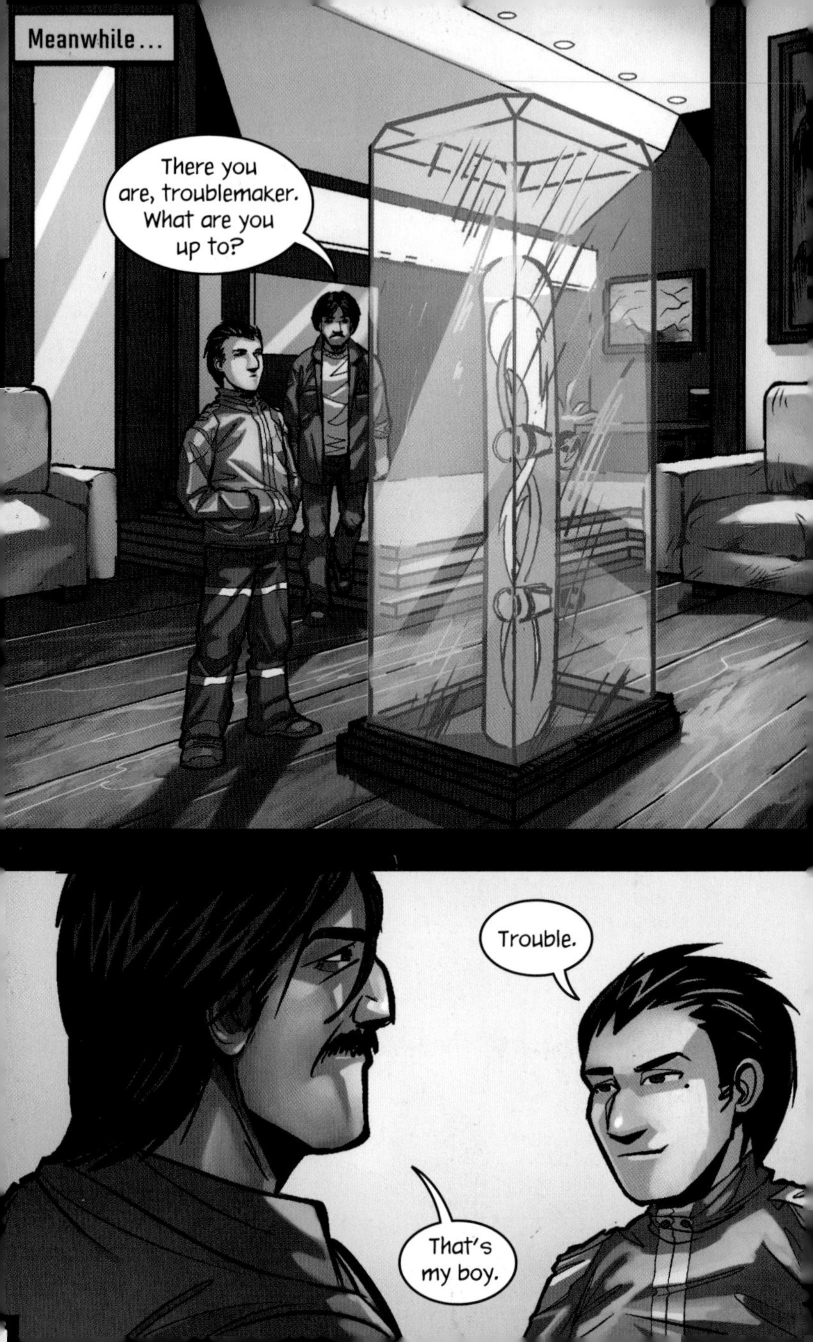
Meanwhile...
There you are, troublemaker. What are you up to?
Trouble.
That's my boy.

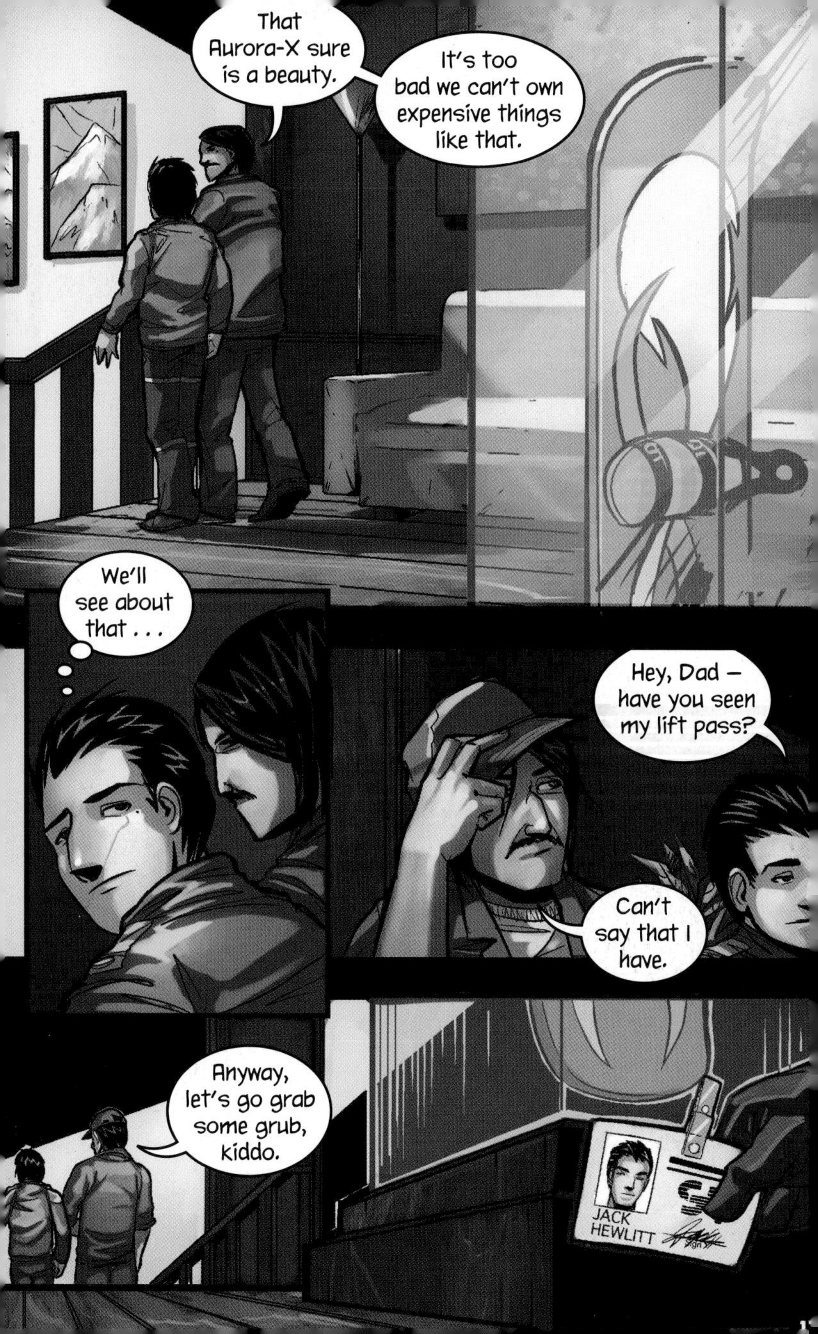
That Aurora-X sure is a beauty.
It's too bad we can't own expensive things like that.
We'll see about that . . .
Hey, Dad — have you seen my lift pass?
Can't say that I have.
Anyway, let's go grab some grub, kiddo.
JACK HEWLITT

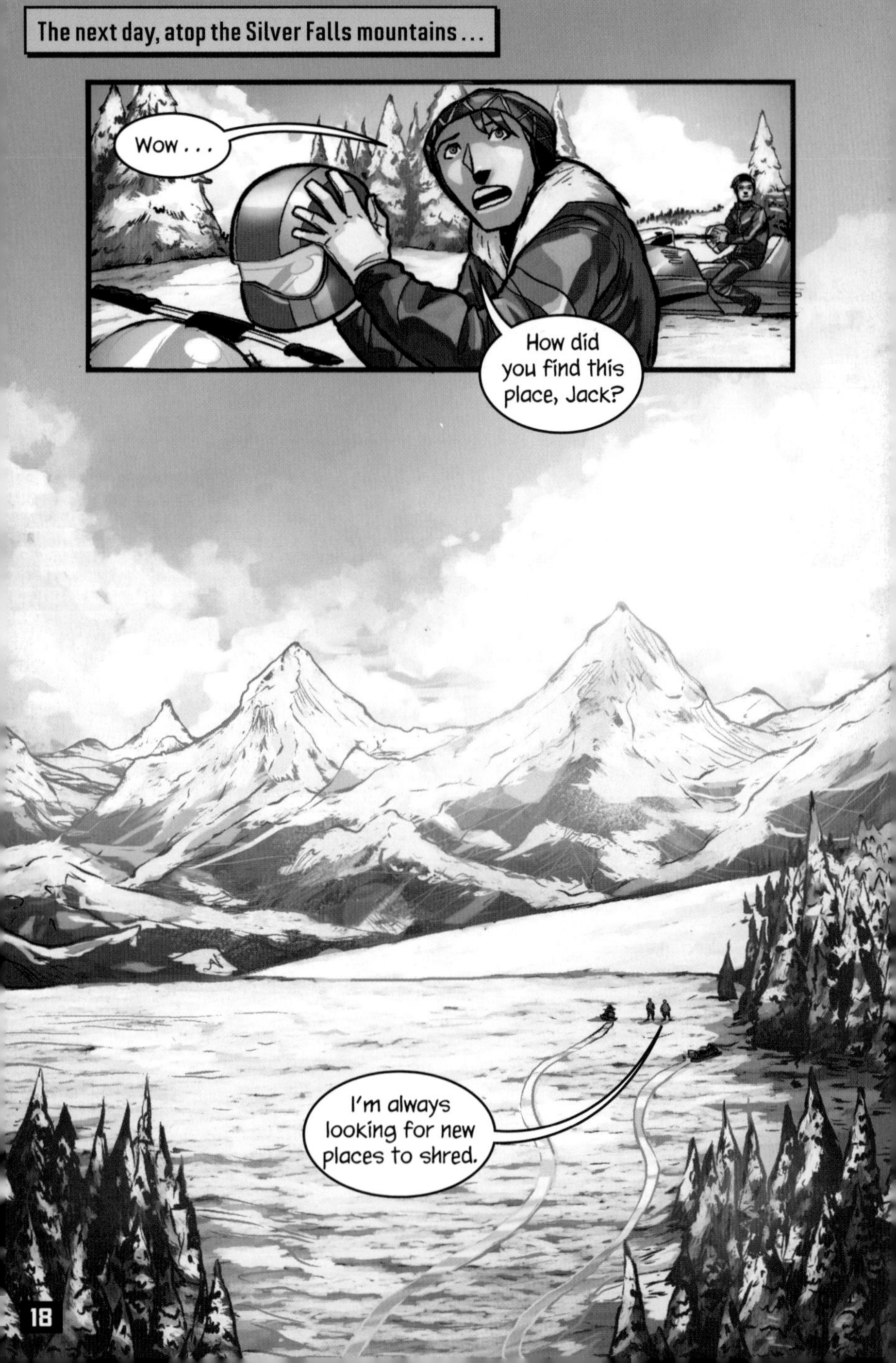
The next day, atop the Silver Falls mountains . . .
Wow . . .
How did you find this place, Jack?
I'm always looking for new places to shred.

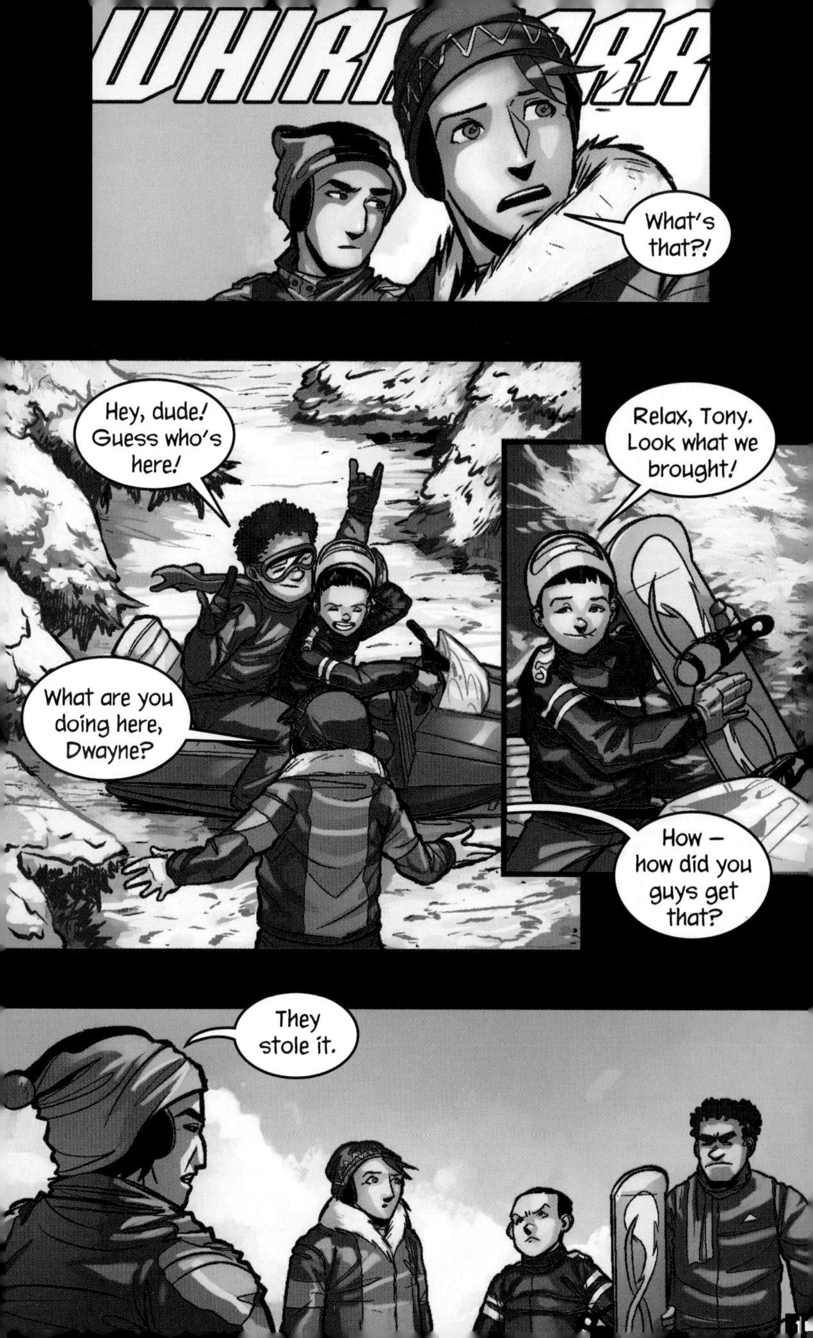
What's that?!
Hey, dude! Guess who's here!
What are you doing here, Dwayne?
Relax, Tony. Look what we brought!
How — how did you guys get that?
They stole it.

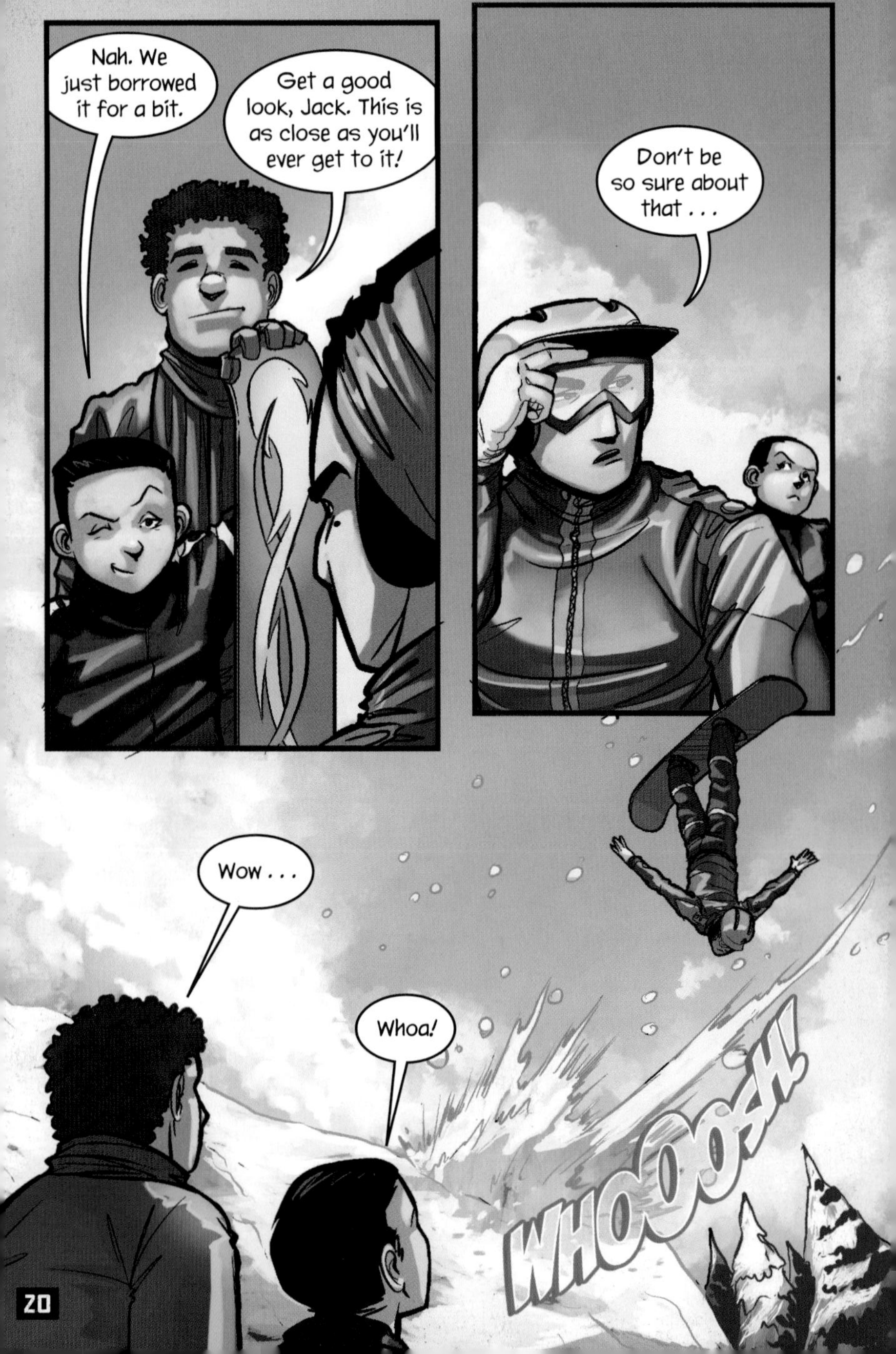
Nah. We just borrowed it for a bit.
Get a good look, Jack. This is as close as you'll ever get to it!
Don't be so sure about that . . .
Wow . . .
Whoa!
WHOOOOSH!

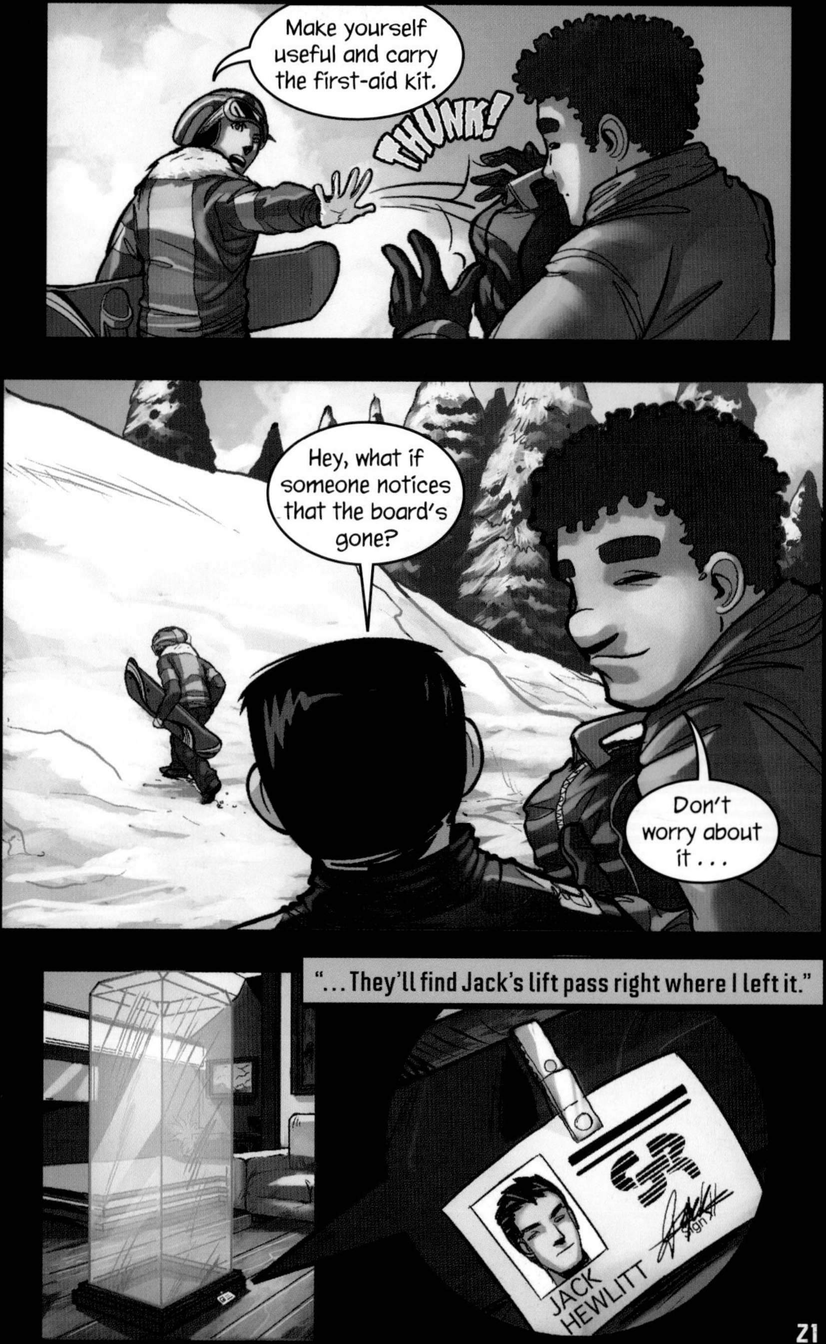
Make yourself useful and carry the first-aid kit.
THUNK!
Hey, what if someone notices that the board's gone?
Don't worry about it . . .
". . . They'll find Jack's lift pass right where I left it."
JACK HEWLITT

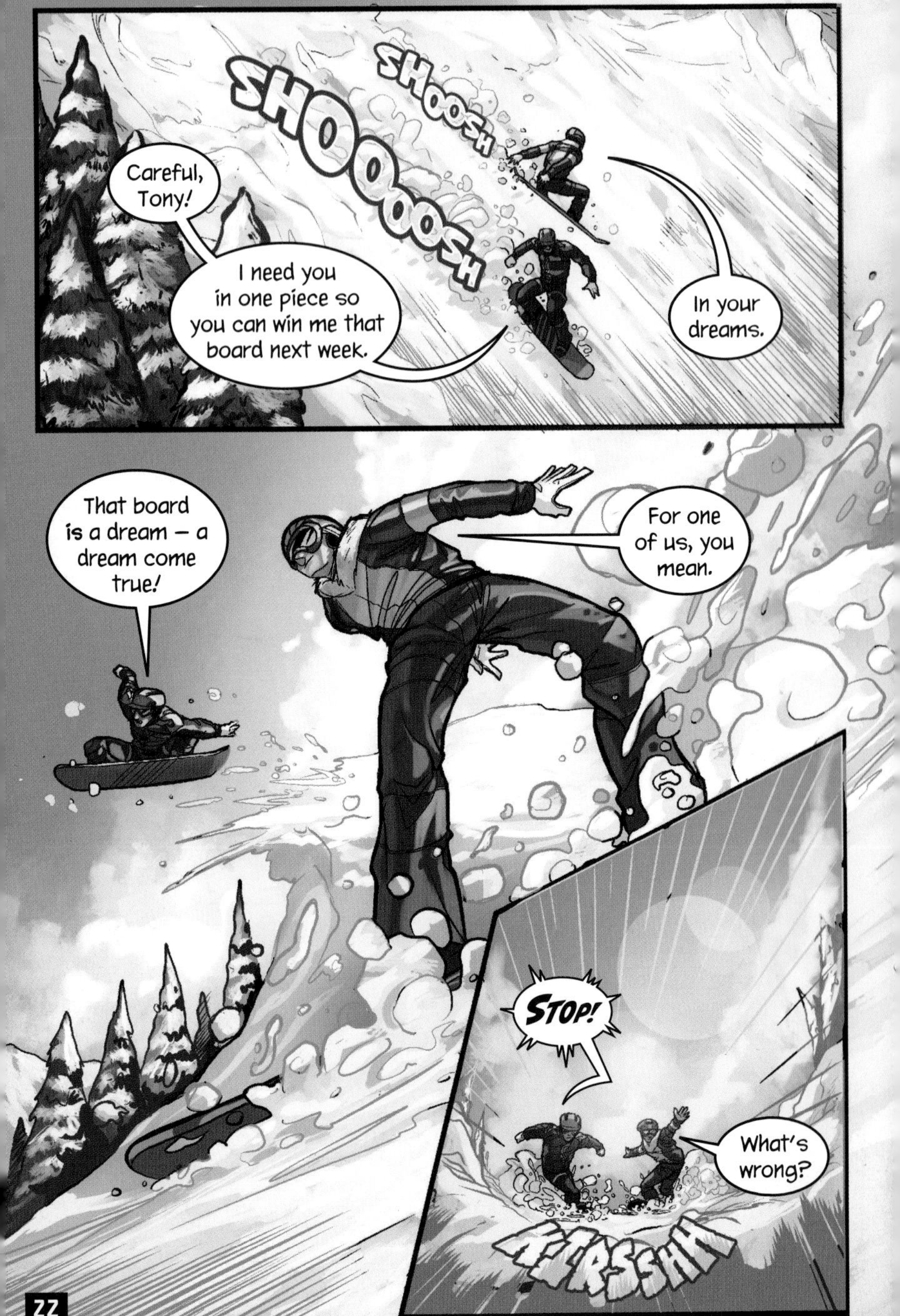
SHOOSH
SHOOOOOSH
Careful, Tony!
I need you in one piece so you can win me that board next week.
In your dreams.
That board is a dream — a dream come true!
For one of us, you mean.
STOP!
What's wrong?

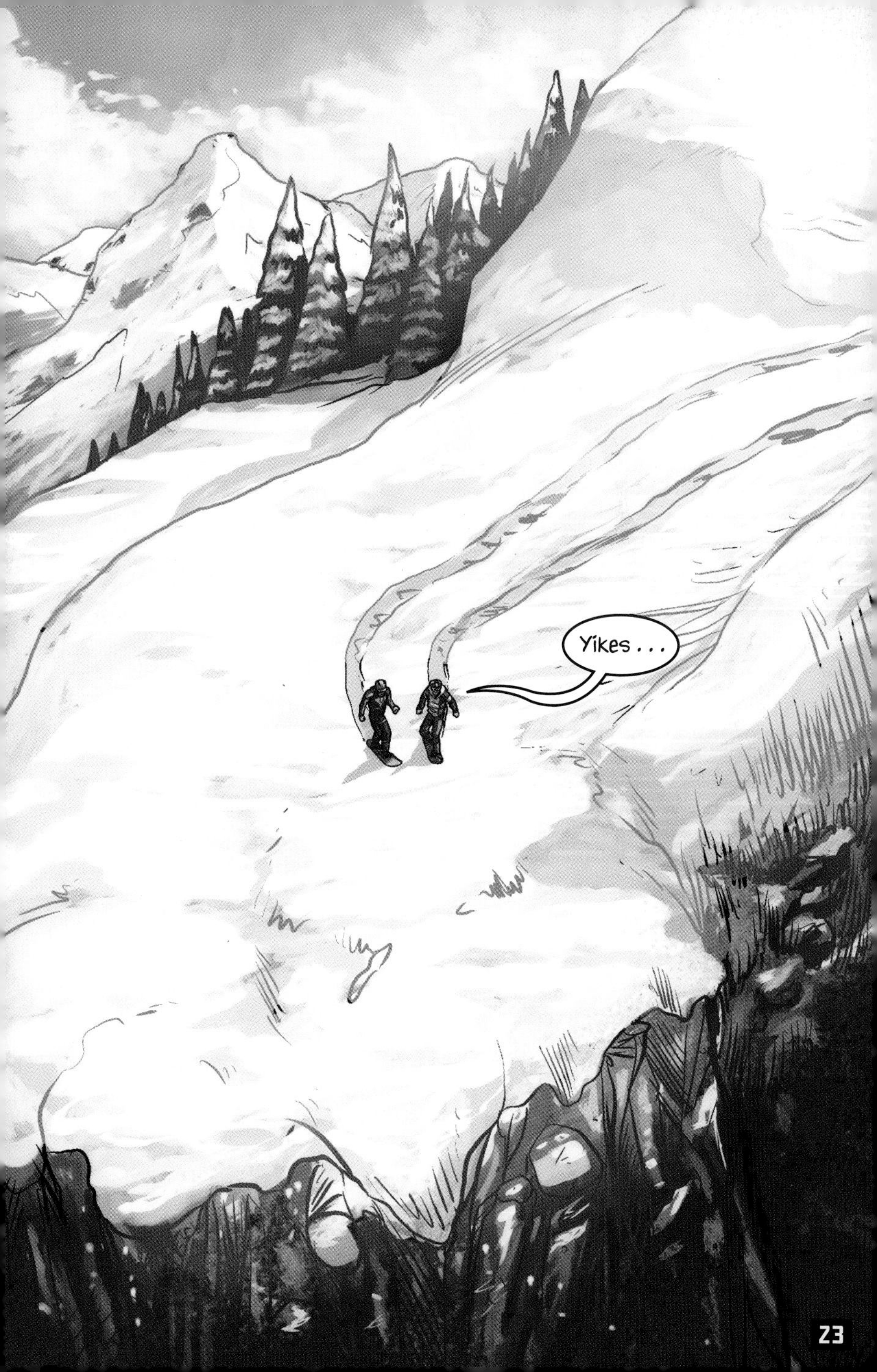
Yikes . . .

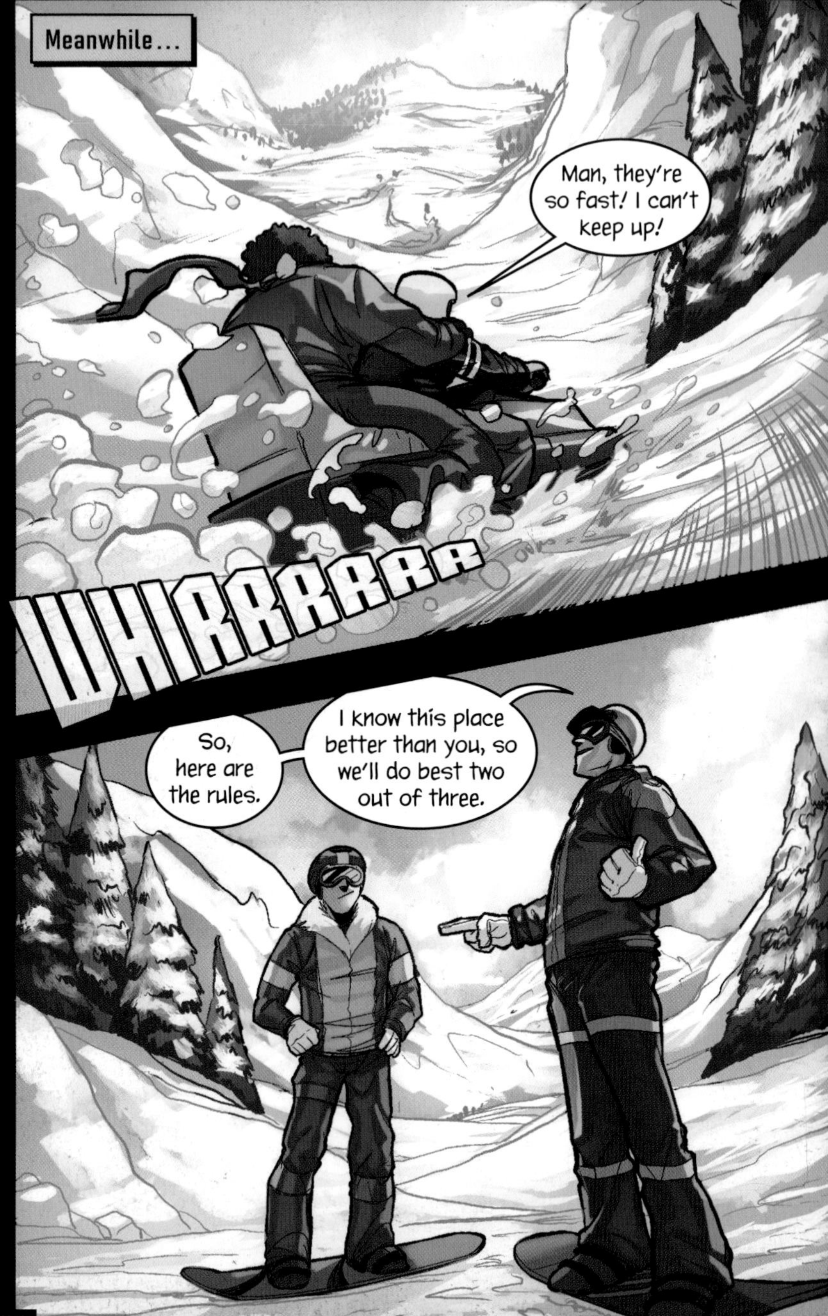
Meanwhile...
Man, they're so fast! I can't keep up!
WHIRRRRRRR
So, here are the rules.
I know this place better than you, so we'll do best two out of three.

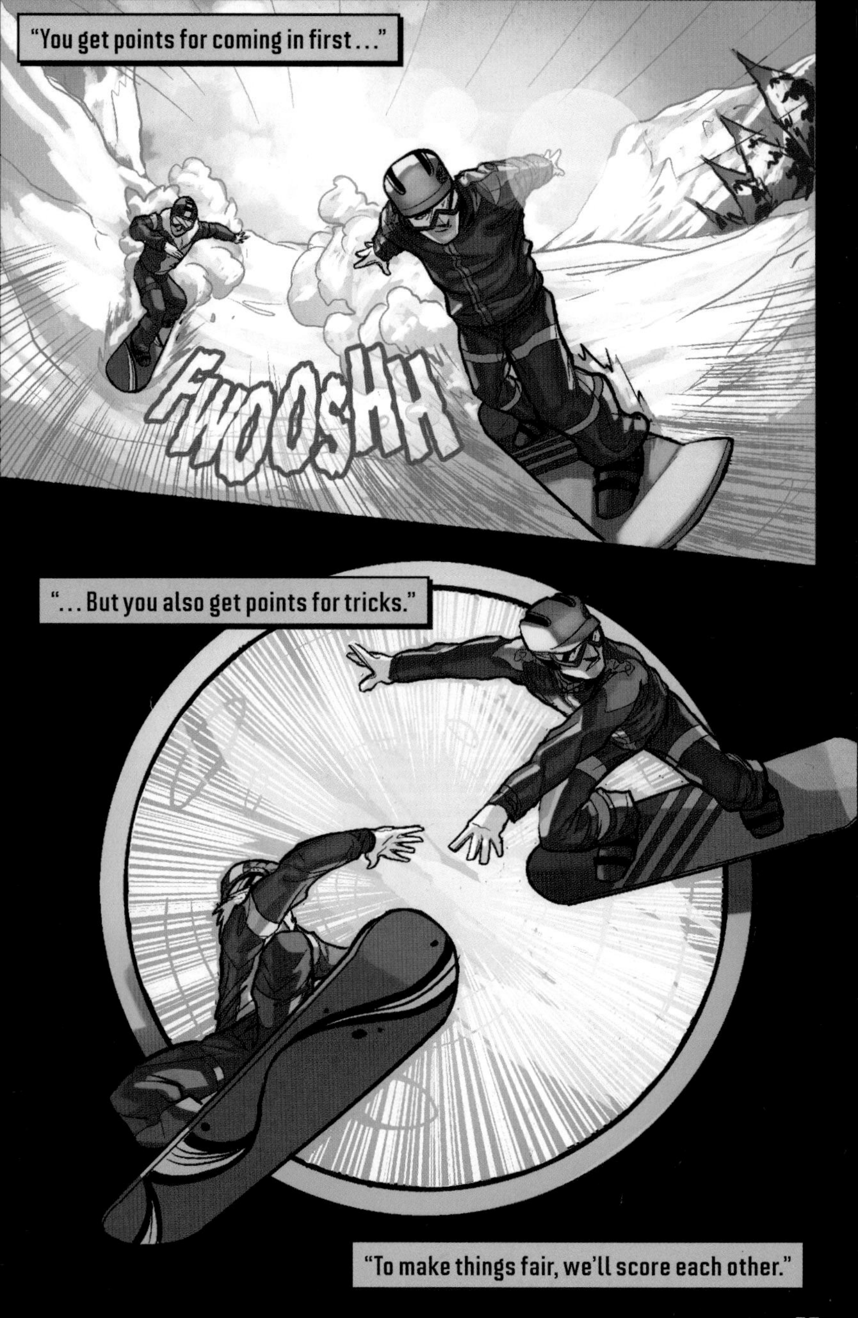
"You get points for coming in first . . ."
FWOOSHA
". . . But you also get points for tricks."
"To make things fair, we'll score each other."

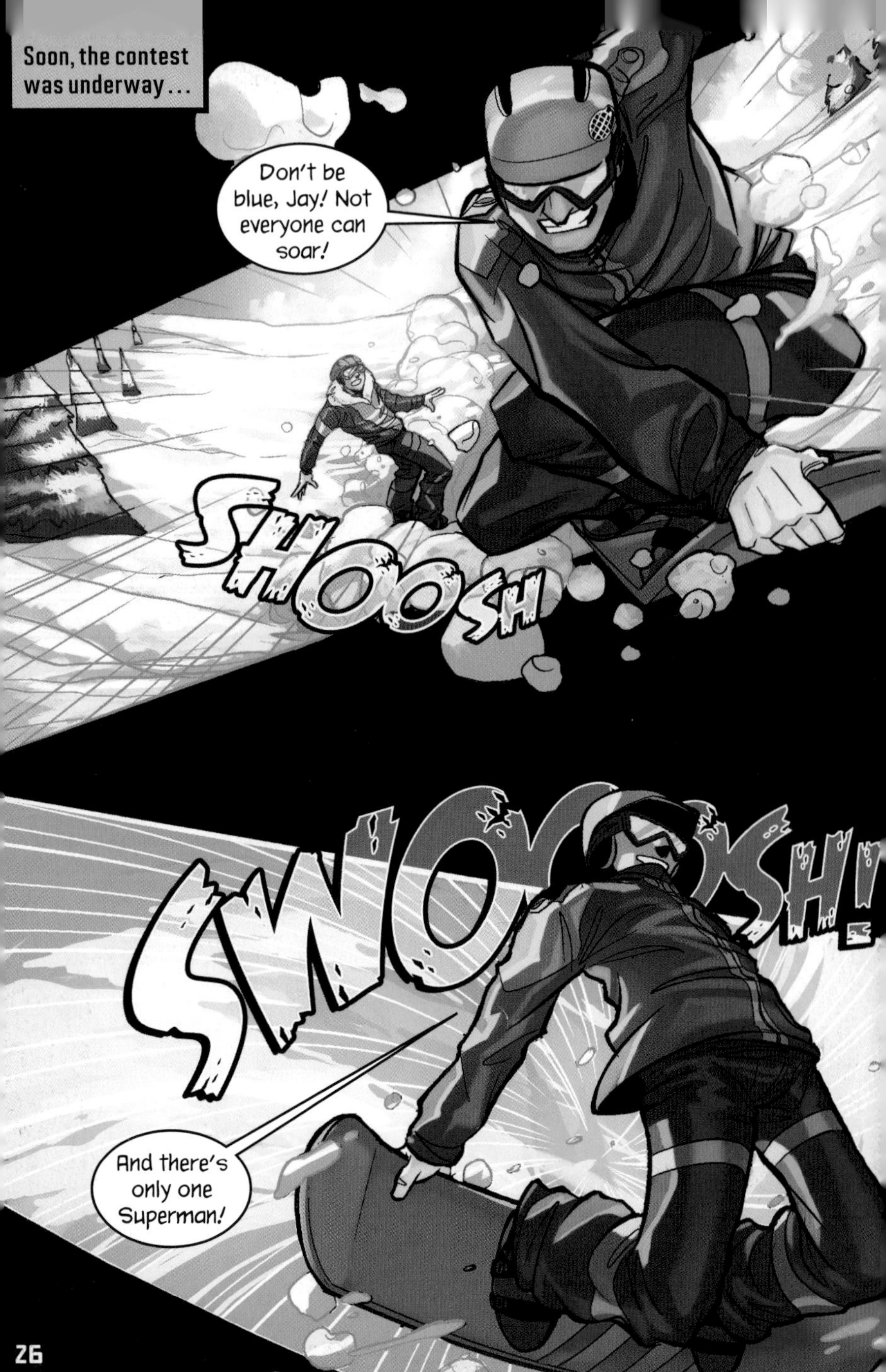
Soon, the contest was underway...
Don't be blue, Jay! Not everyone can soar!
SHOOSH
SWOOOSH!
And there's only one Superman!

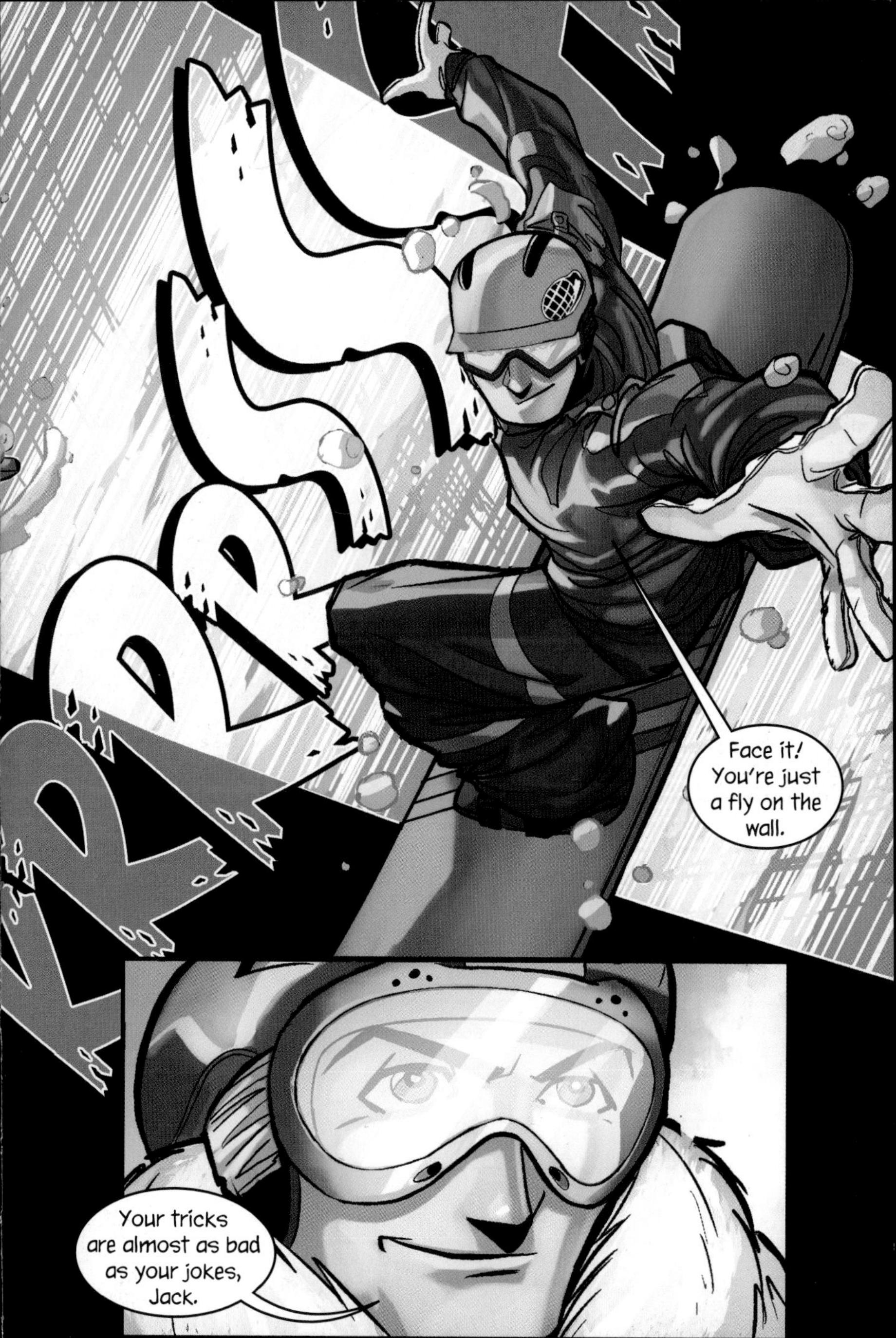
Face it! You're just a fly on the wall.
Your tricks are almost as bad as your jokes, Jack.

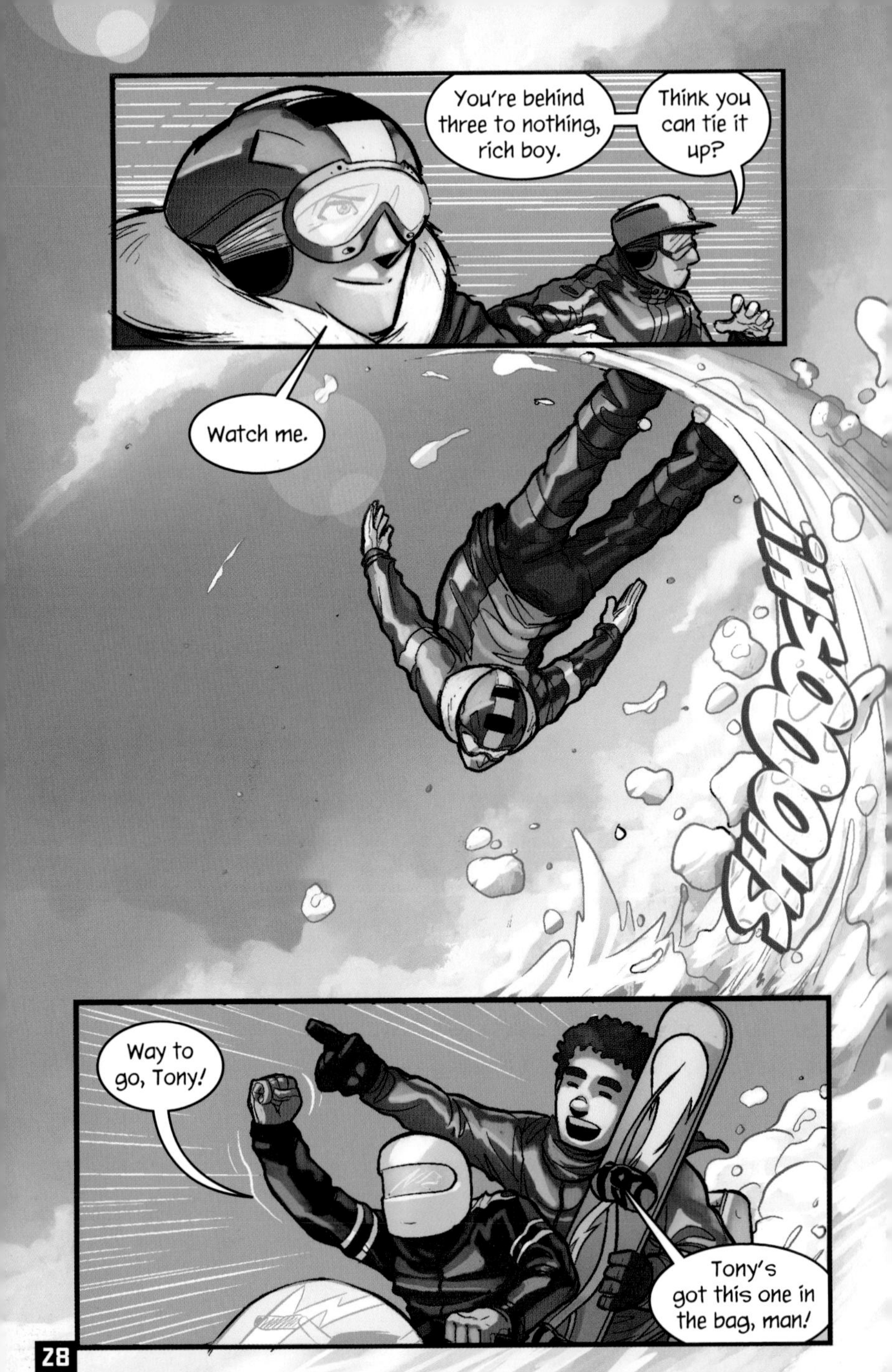
You're behind three to nothing, rich boy.
Think you can tie it up?
Watch me.
SHOOOSH!
Way to go, Tony!
Tony's got this one in the bag, man!

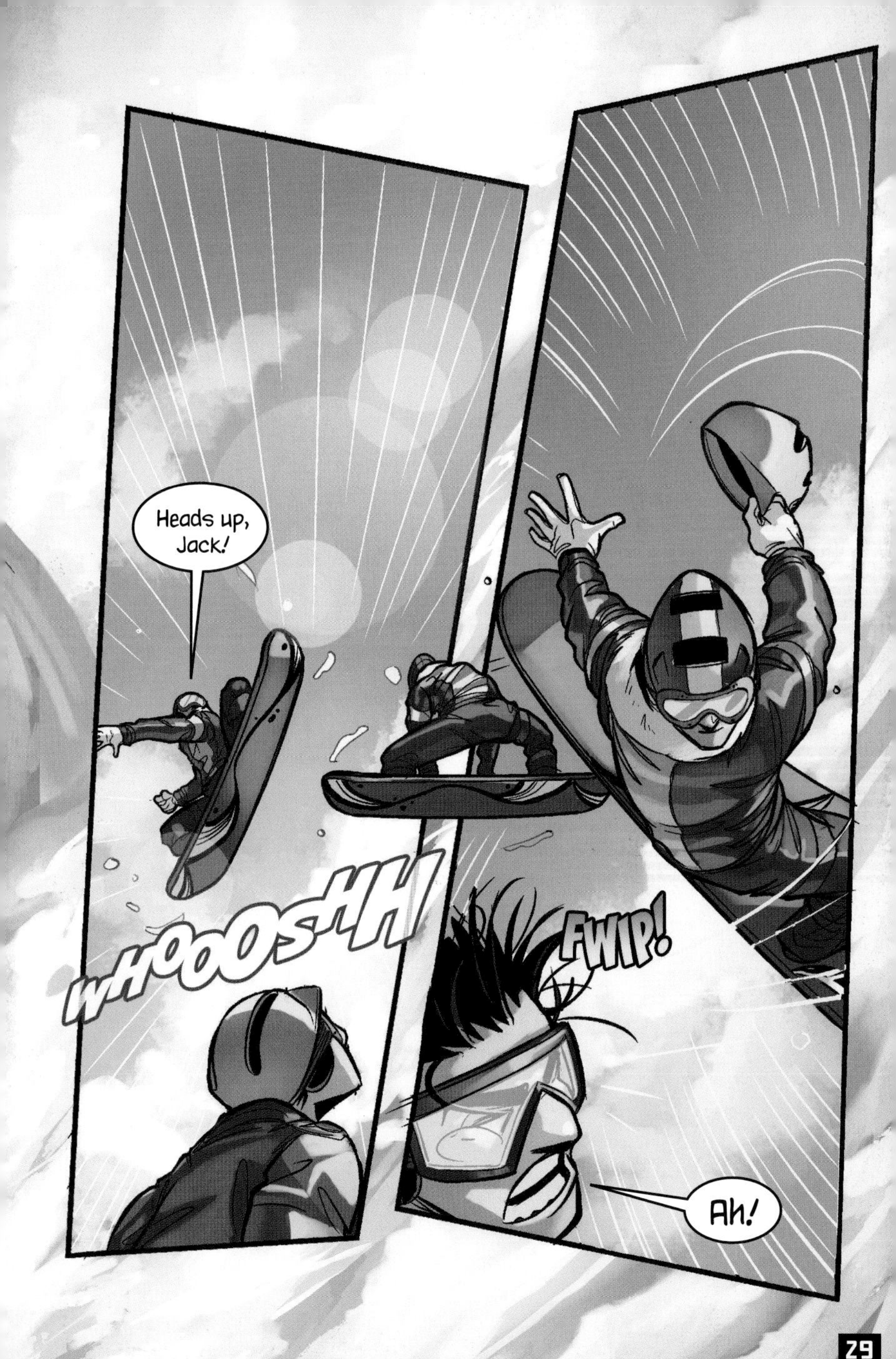
Heads up, Jack!
WHOOOOSHH!
FWIP!
Ah!

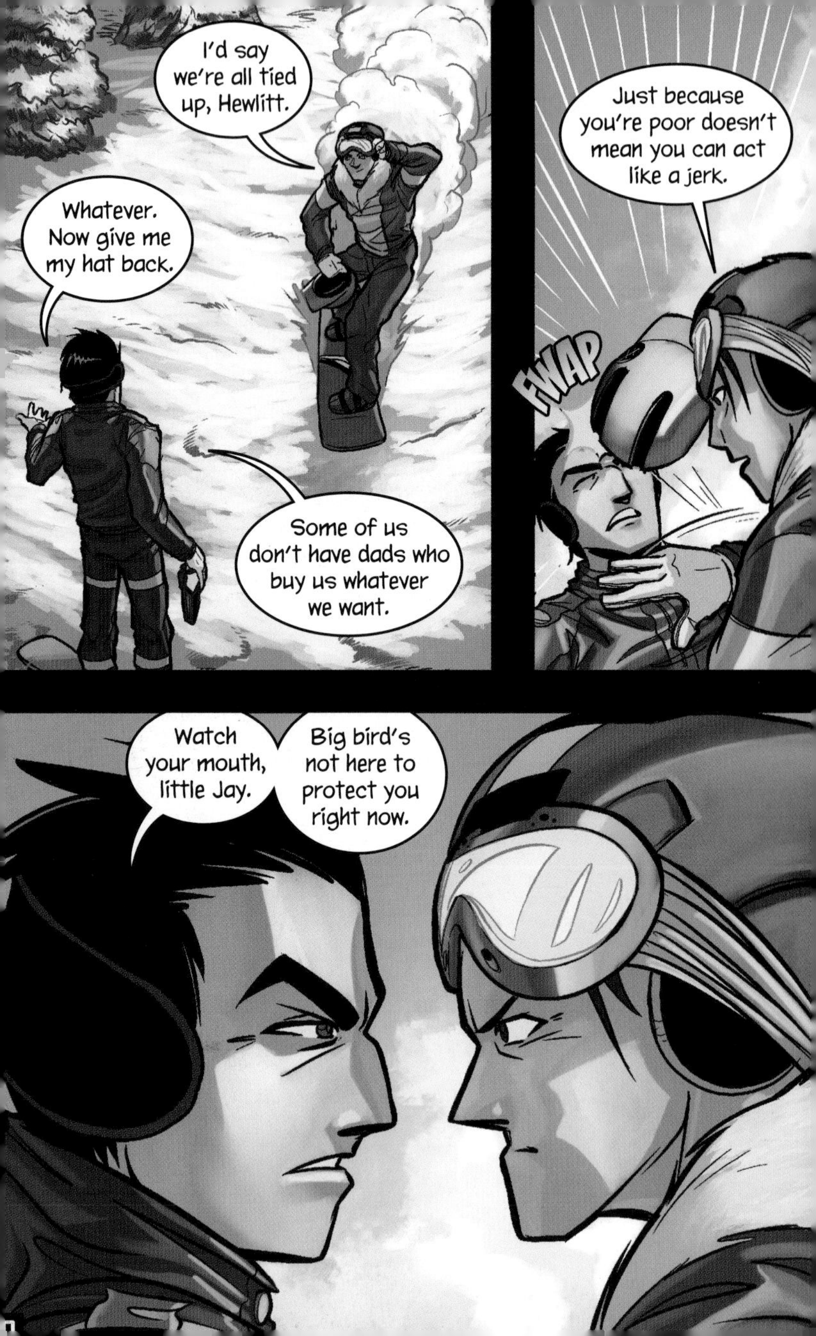
I'd say we're all tied up, Hewlitt.
Whatever. Now give me my hat back.
Some of us don't have dads who buy us whatever we want.
Just because you're poor doesn't mean you can act like a jerk.
FWAP
Watch your mouth, little Jay.
Big bird's not here to protect you right now.

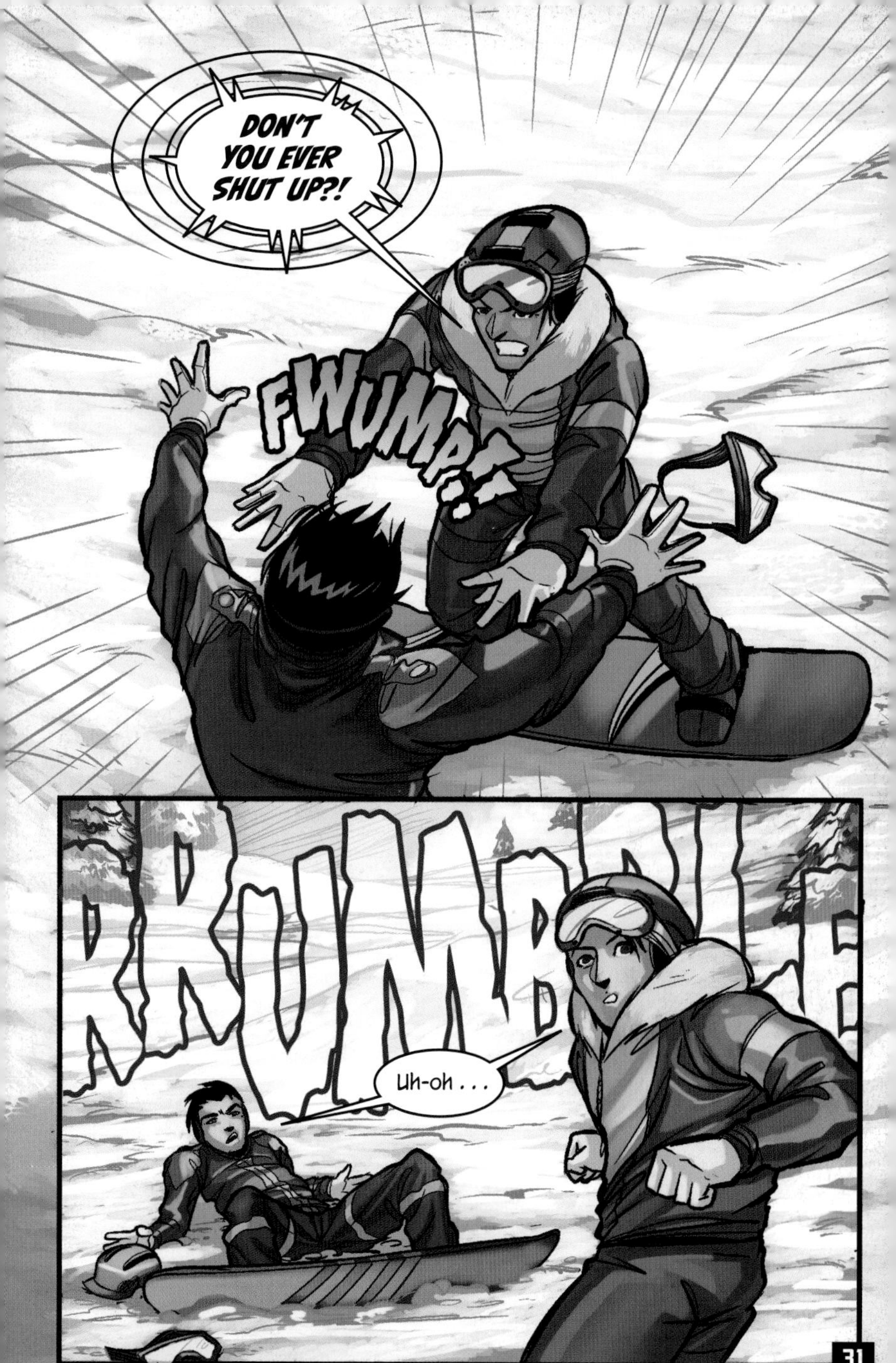
DON'T YOU EVER SHUT UP?!
FWUMP!!
RRUMBLE
Uh-oh . . .

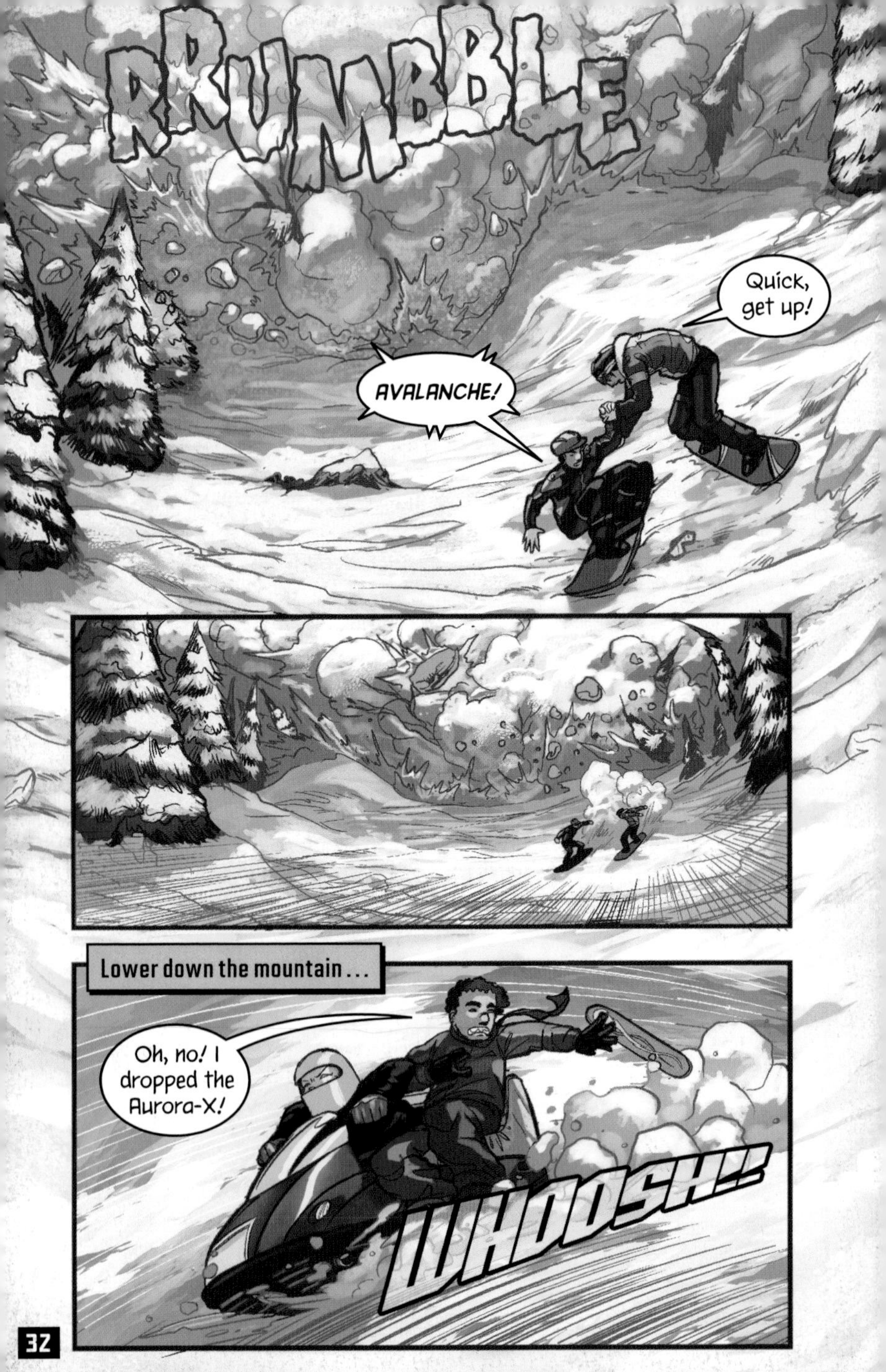
RRUMBLE
Quick, get up!
AVALANCHE!
Lower down the mountain . . .
Oh, no! I dropped the Aurora-X!
WHOOSH!!

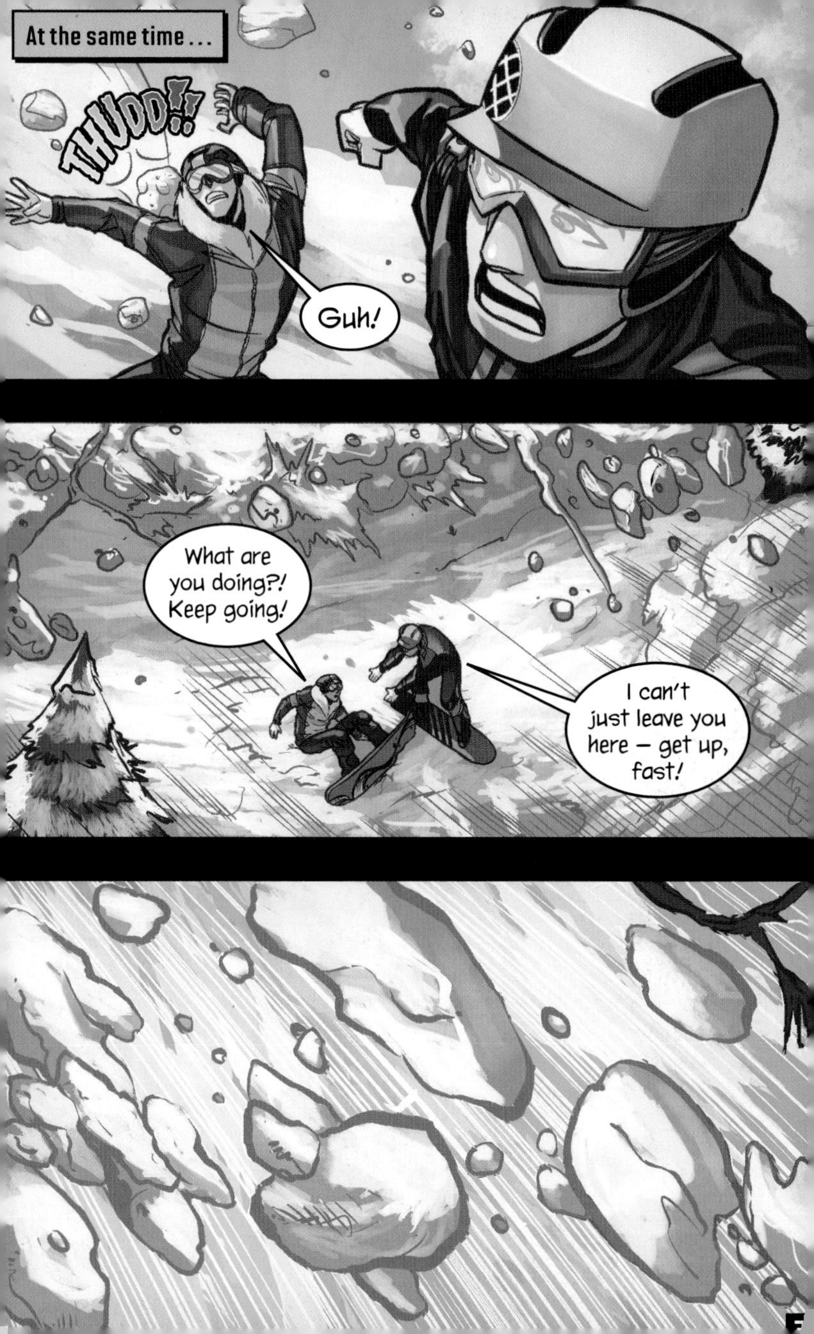
At the same time . . .
THUDD!!!
Guh!
What are you doing?! Keep going!
I can't just leave you here — get up, fast!

FWOOSH!

Dwayne, stop — help me find Tony!
No way! You're on your own!

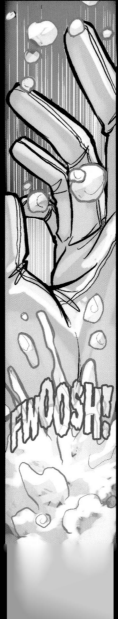

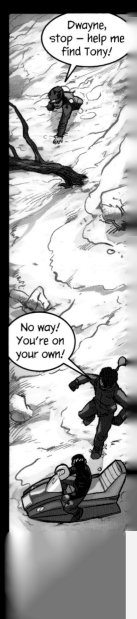

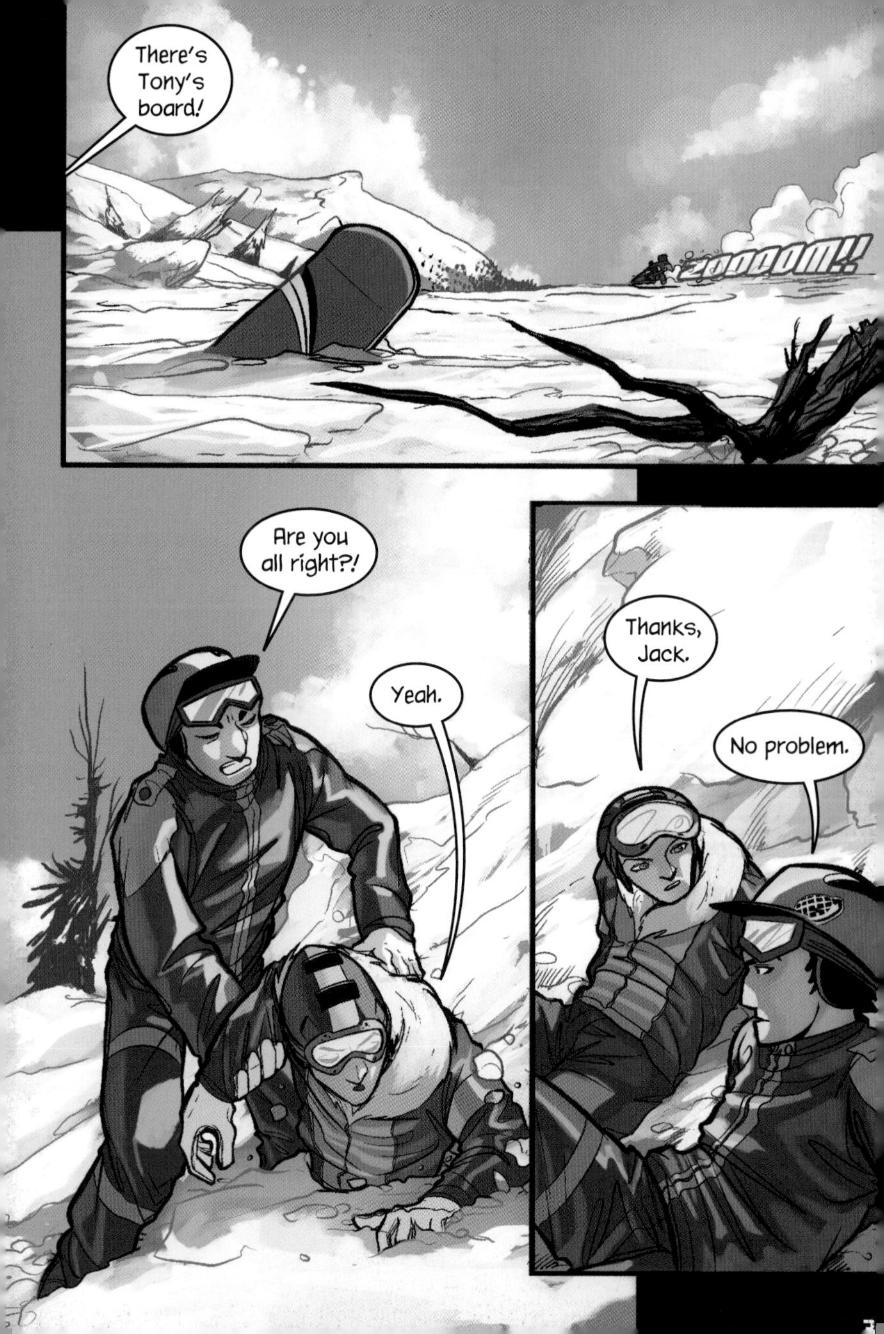
There's Tony's board!
ZOOOOOM!!
Are you all right?!
Yeah.
Thanks, Jack.
No problem.

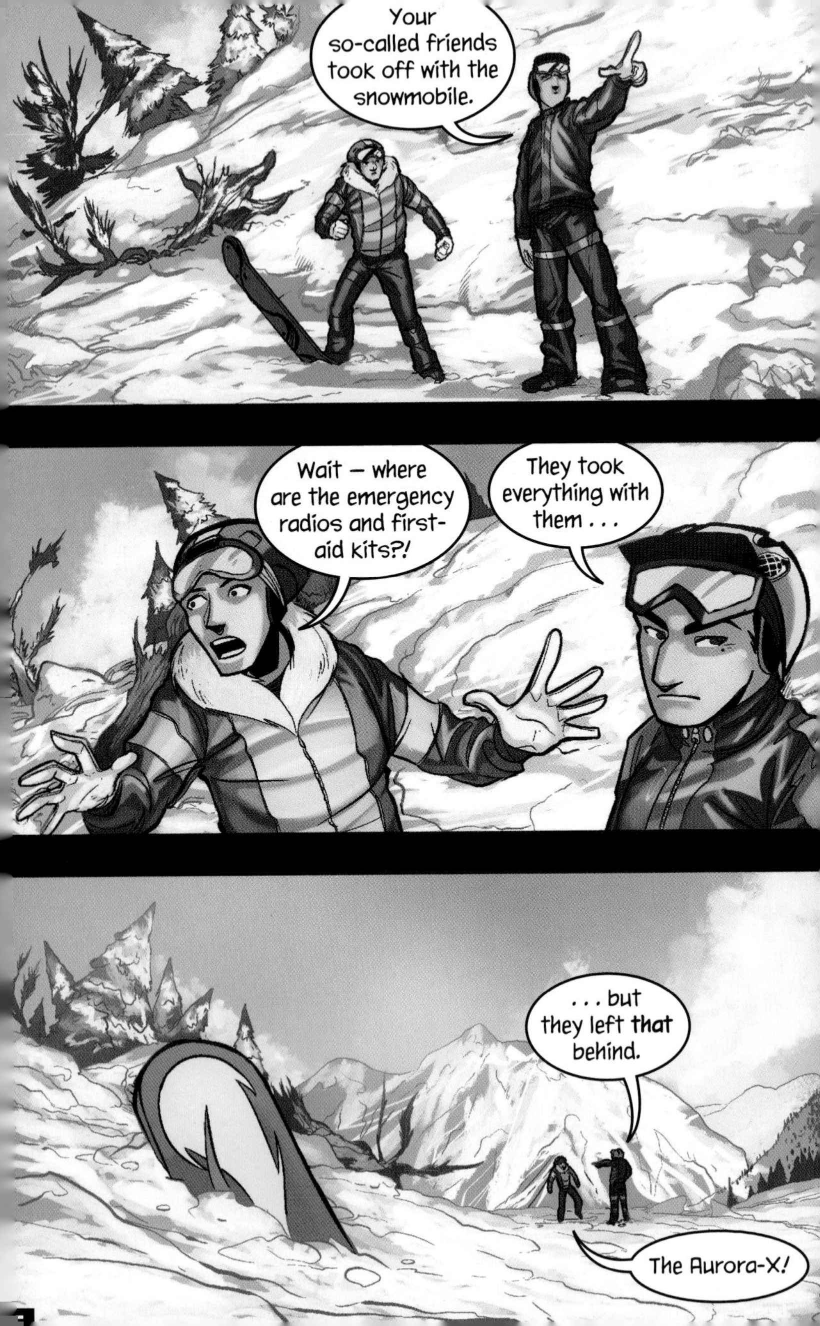
Your so-called friends took off with the snowmobile.
Wait — where are the emergency radios and first-aid kits?!
They took everything with them . . .
. . . but they left that behind.
The Aurora-X!

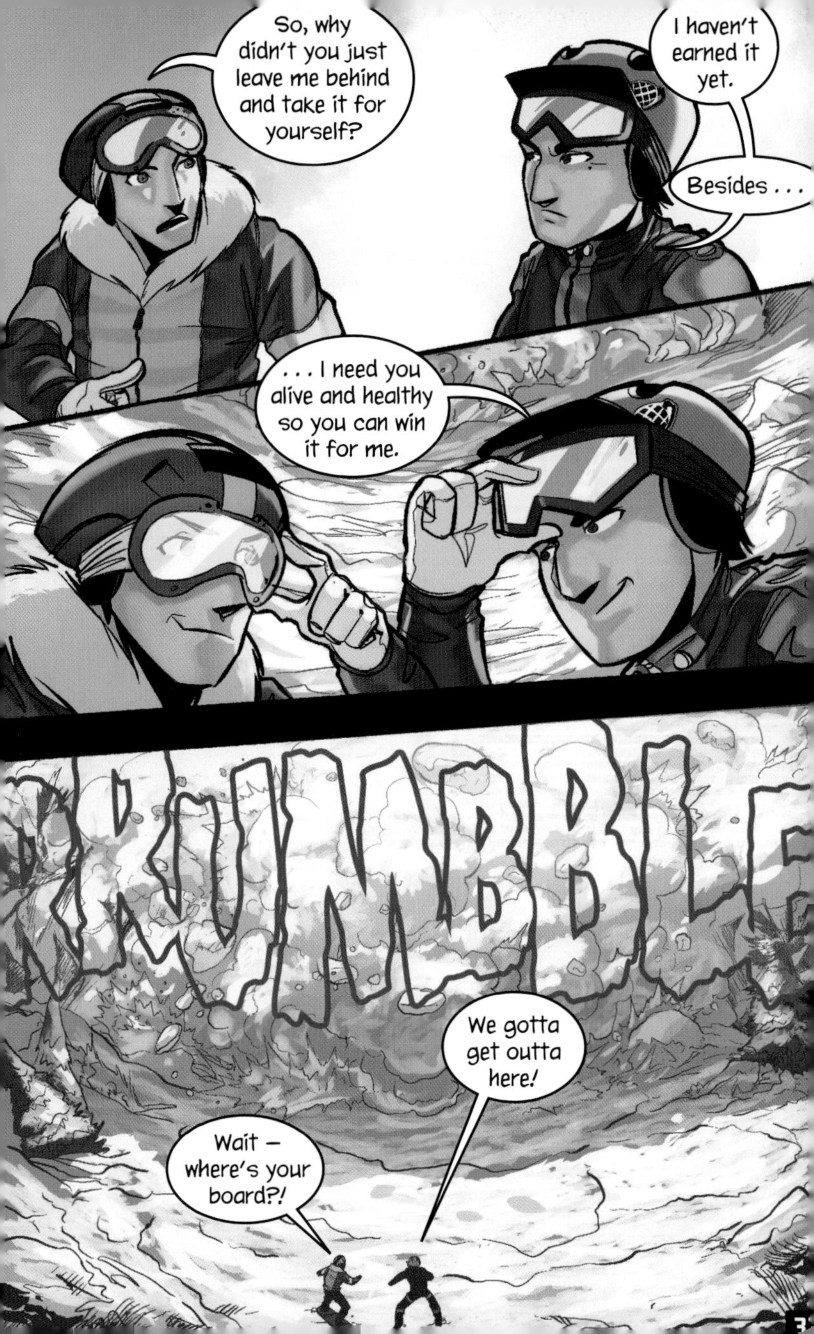
So, why didn't you just leave me behind and take it for yourself?
I haven't earned it yet.
Besides . . .
. . . I need you alive and healthy so you can win it for me.
RUMBLE
We gotta get outta here!
Wait — where's your board?!

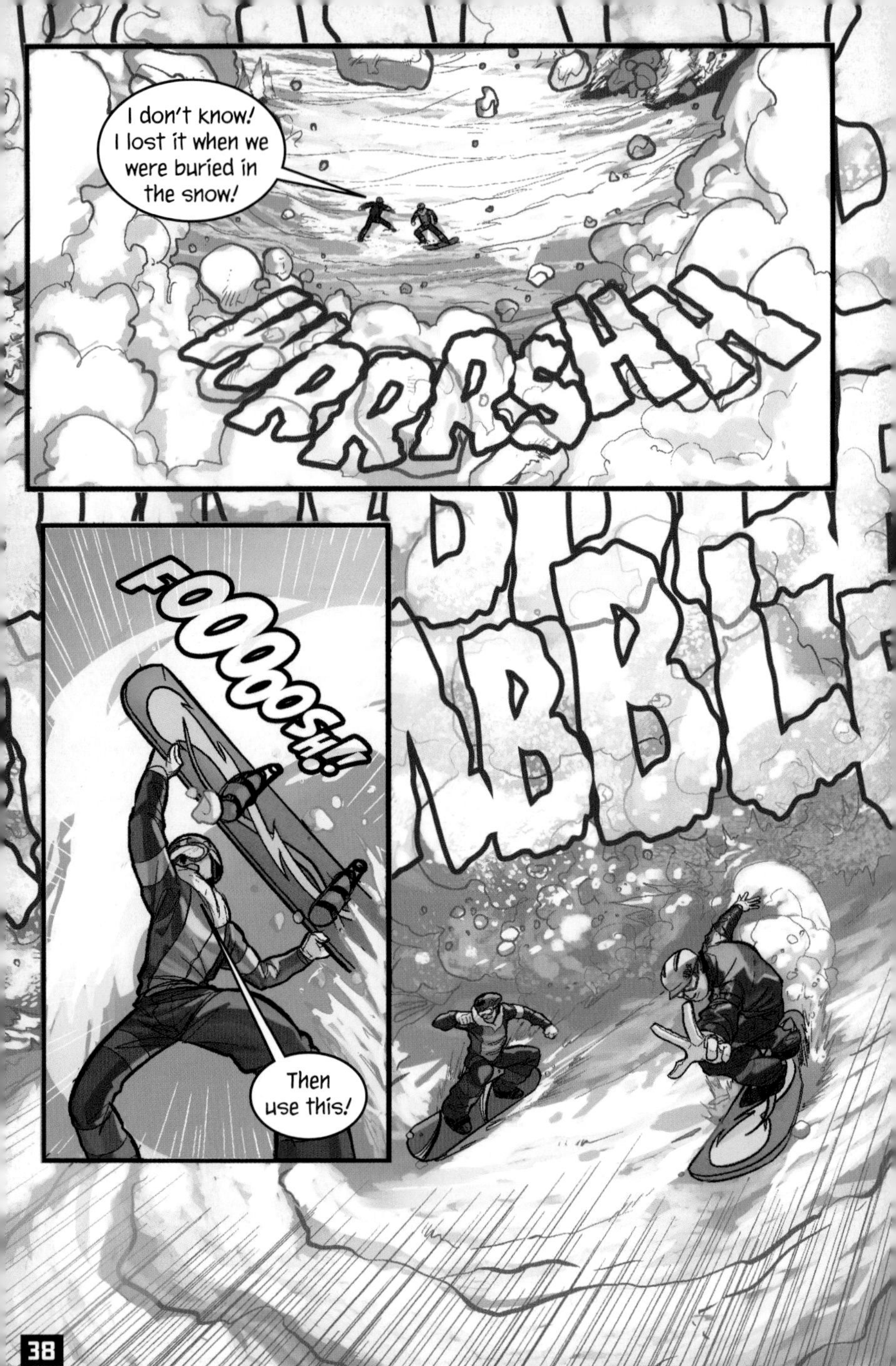
I don't know! I lost it when we were buried in the snow!
KRRRSHH
FOOOOOSH!!
Then use this!

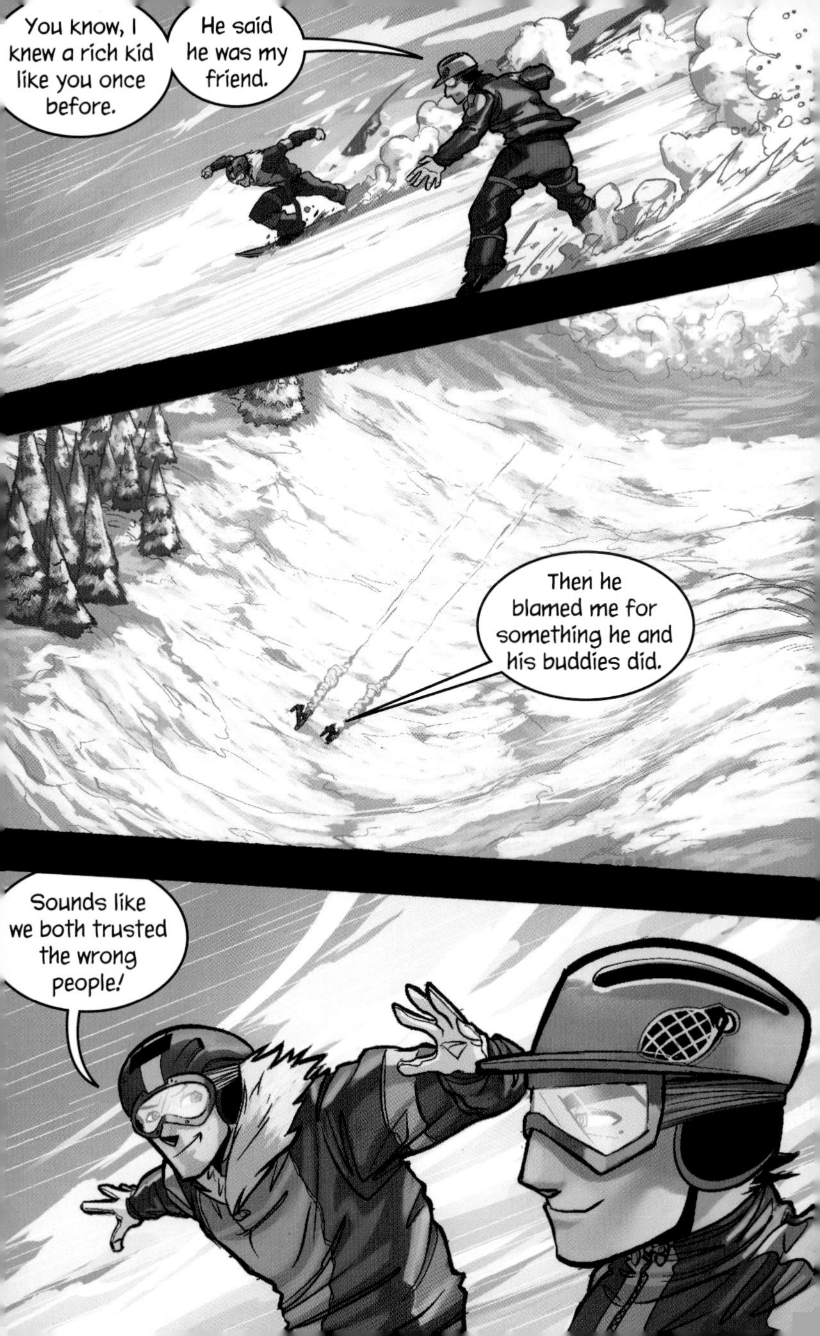
You know, I knew a rich kid like you once before.
He said he was my friend.
Then he blamed me for something he and his buddies did.
Sounds like we both trusted the wrong people!

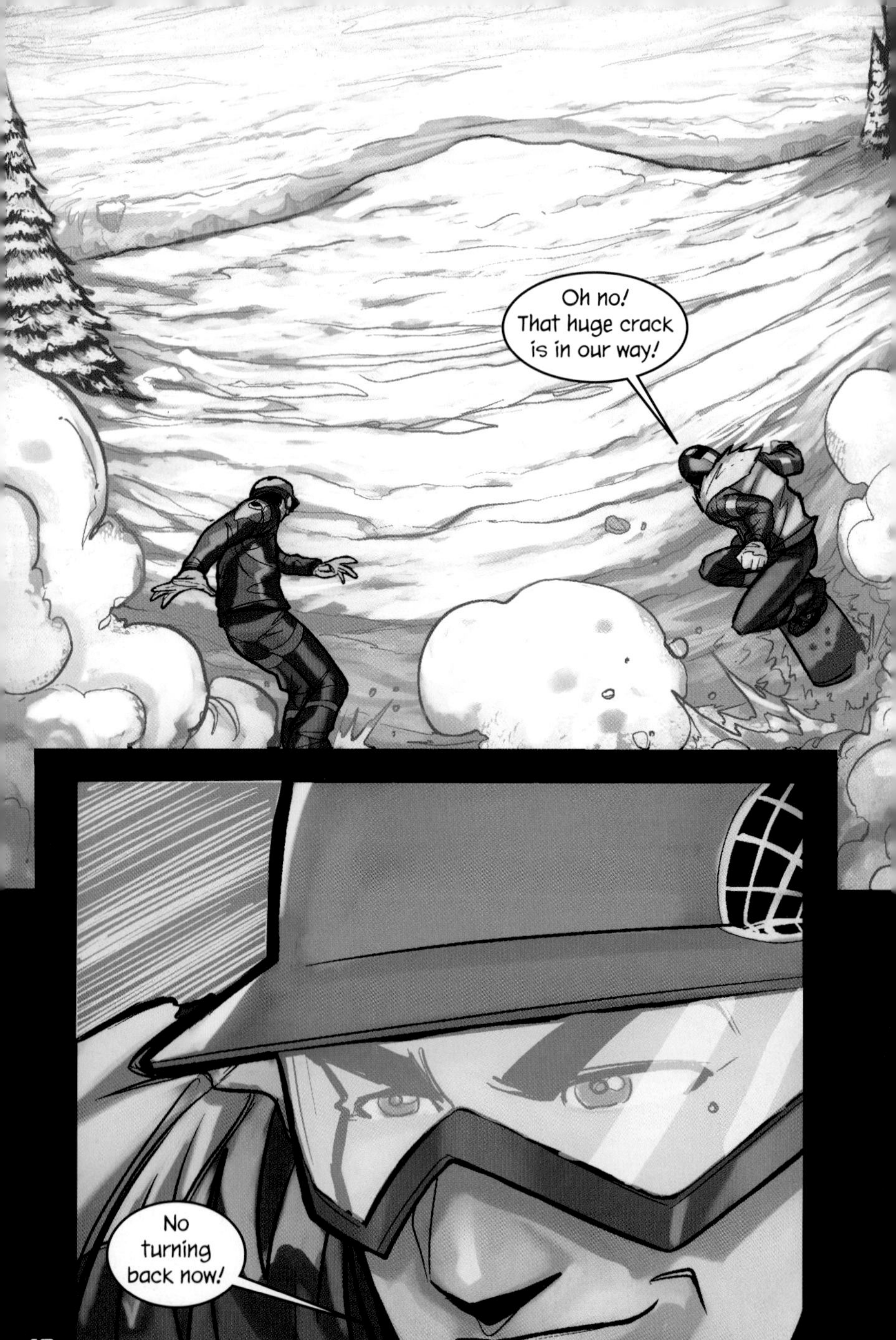
Oh no! That huge crack is in our way!
No turning back now!

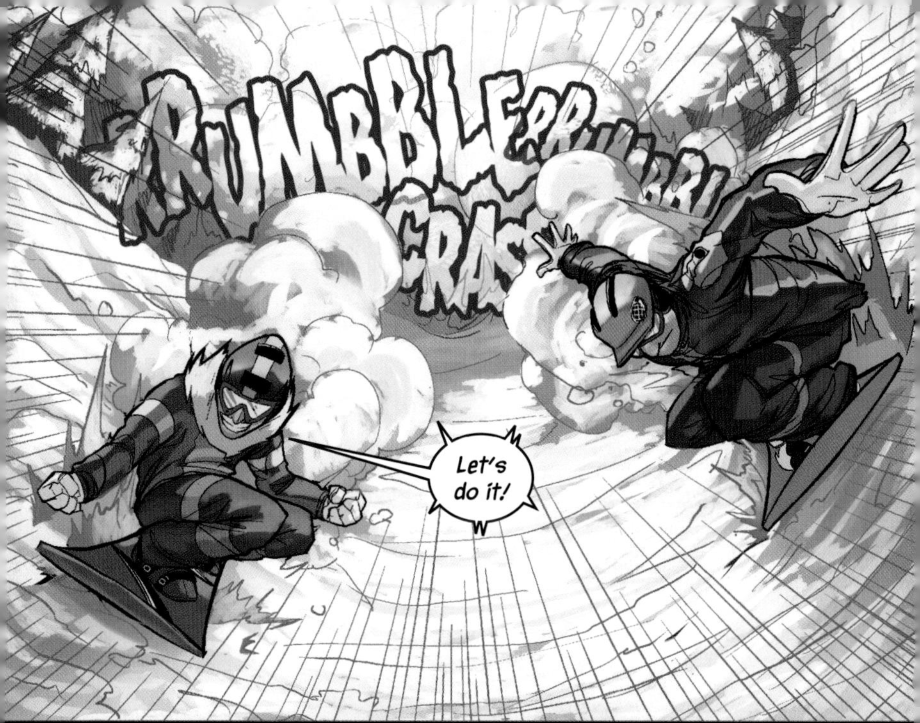
RUMBBLE
Let's do it!

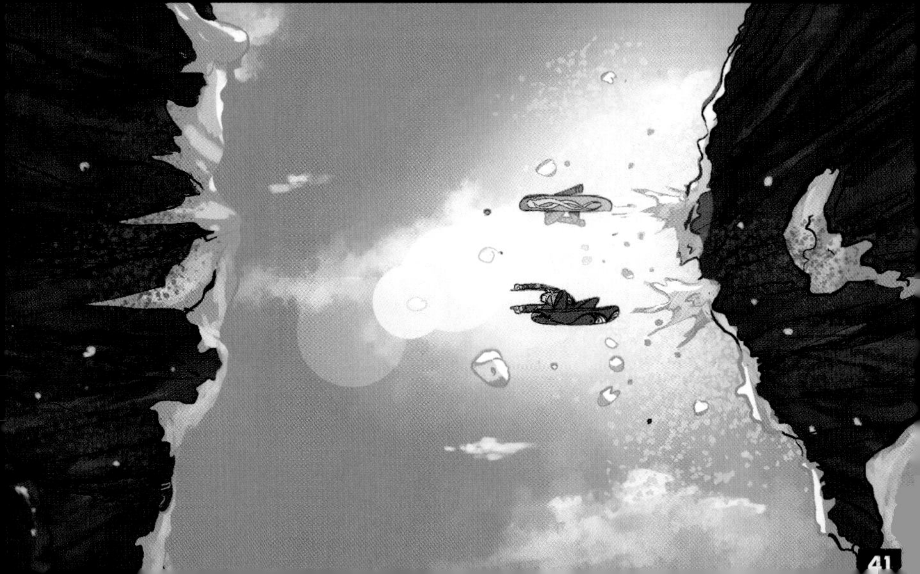

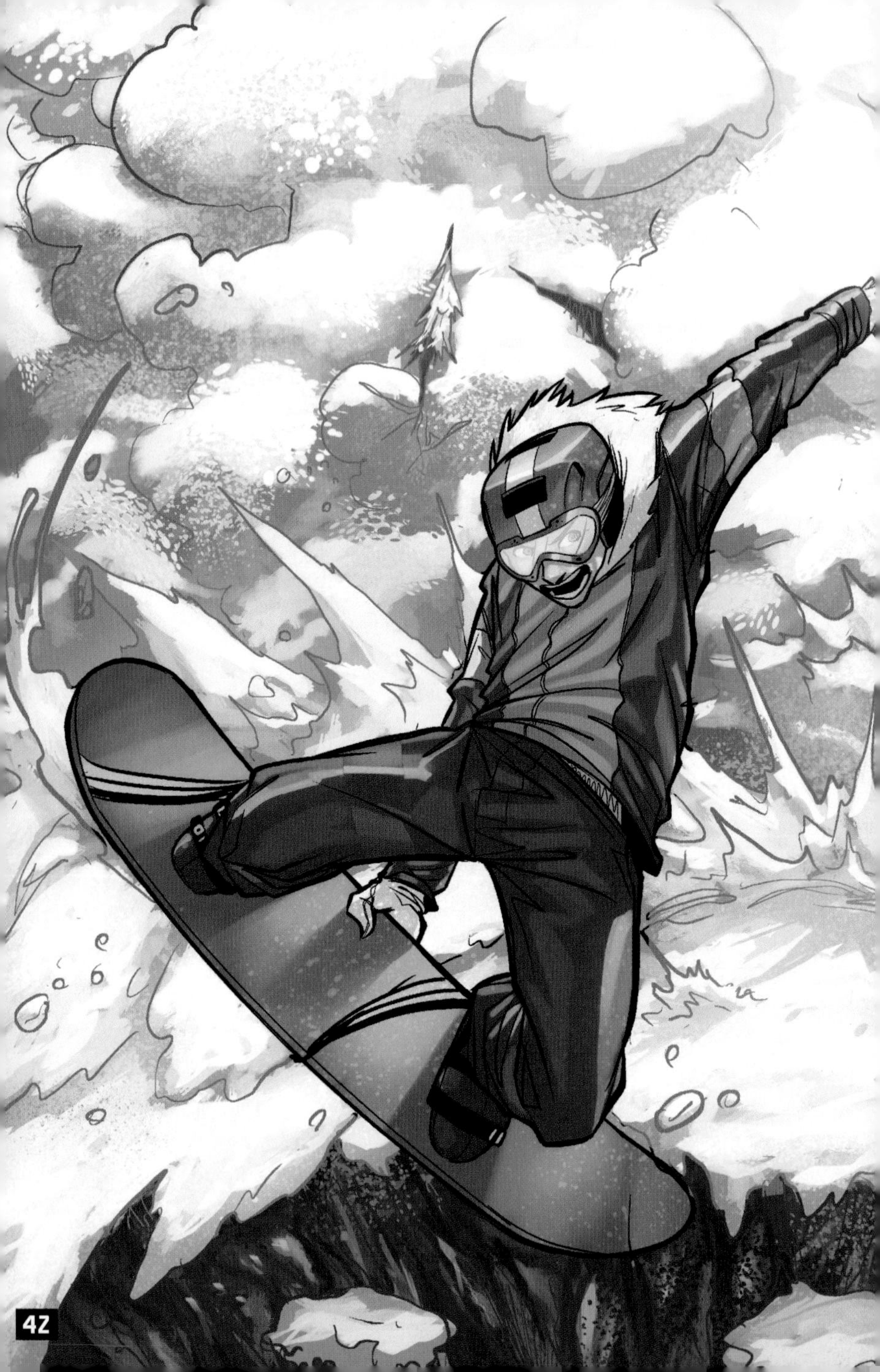

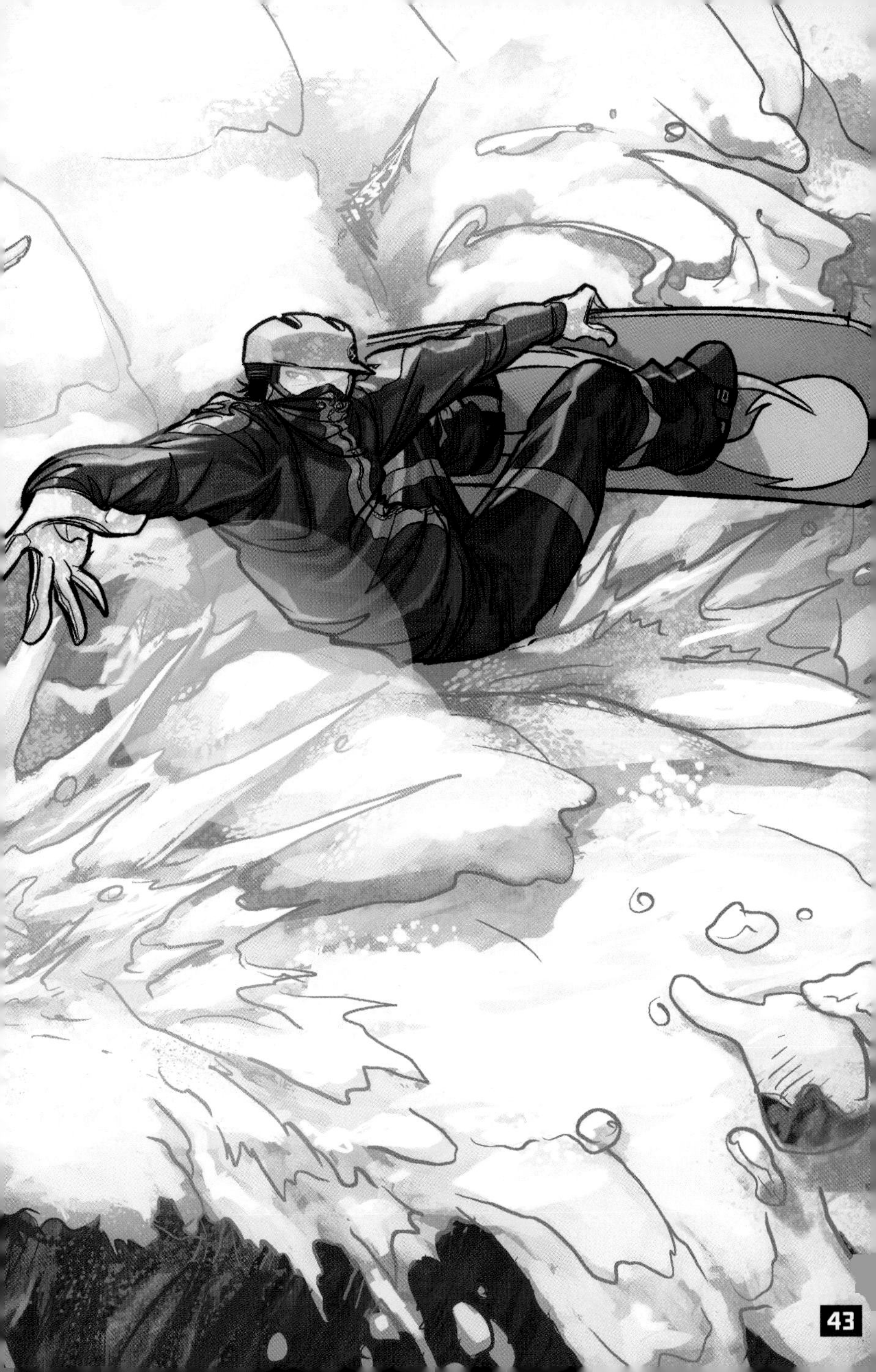

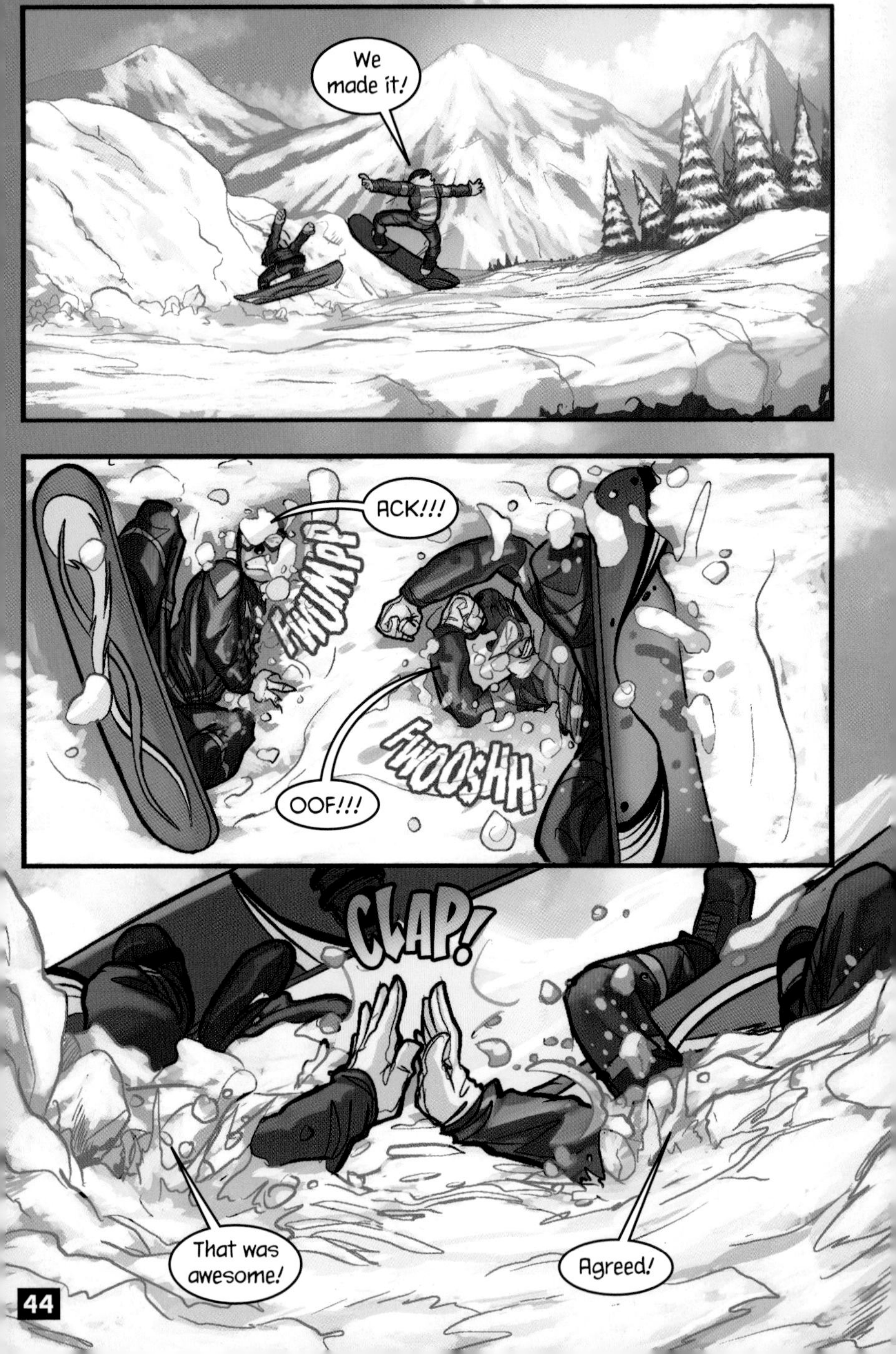

We made it!
ACK!!!
FWUMP
FWOOSHH
OOF!!!
CLAP!
That was awesome!
Agreed!

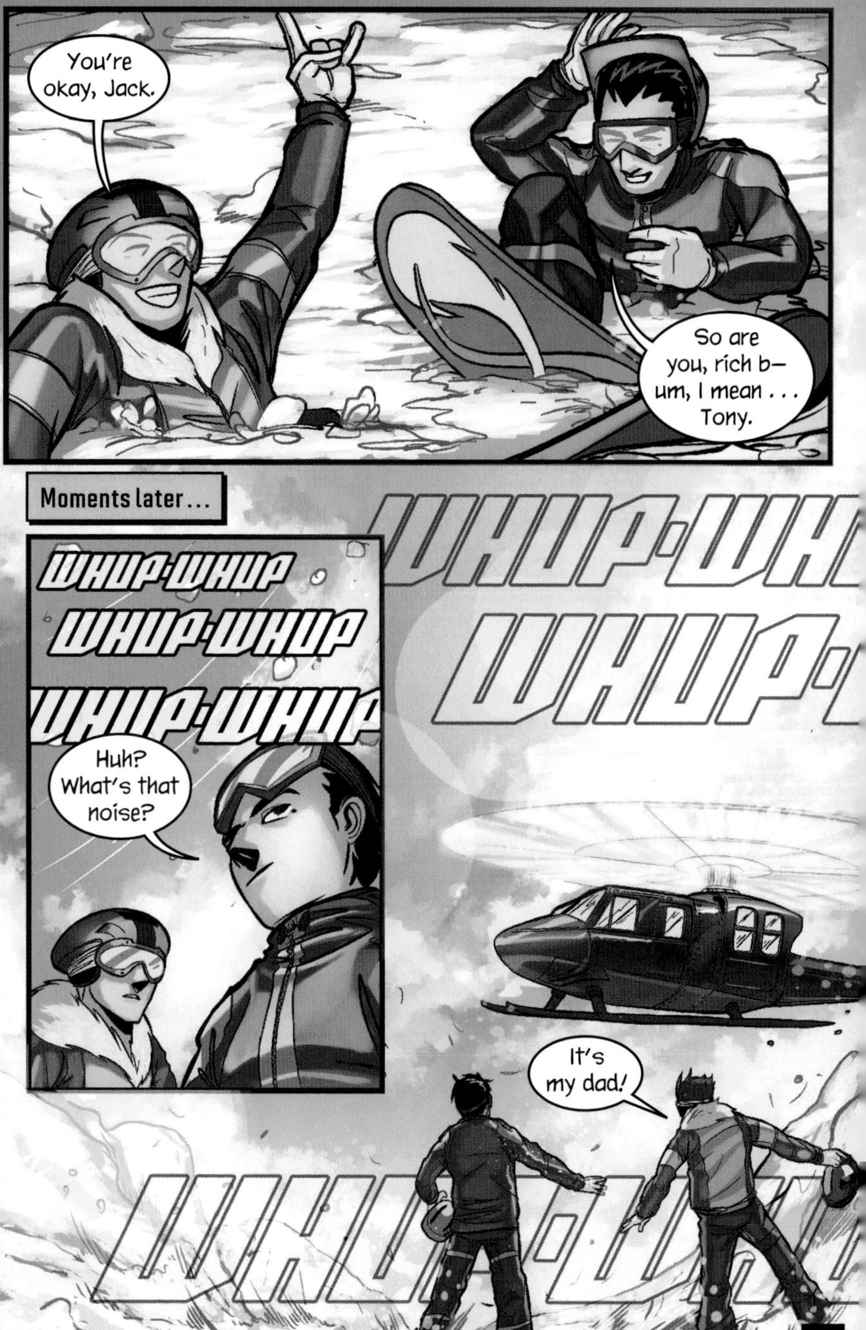

You're okay, Jack.
So are you, rich b— um, I mean . . . Tony.
Moments later . . .
WHUP-WHUP
WHUP-WHUP
WHUP-WHUP
Huh? What's that noise?
It's my dad!

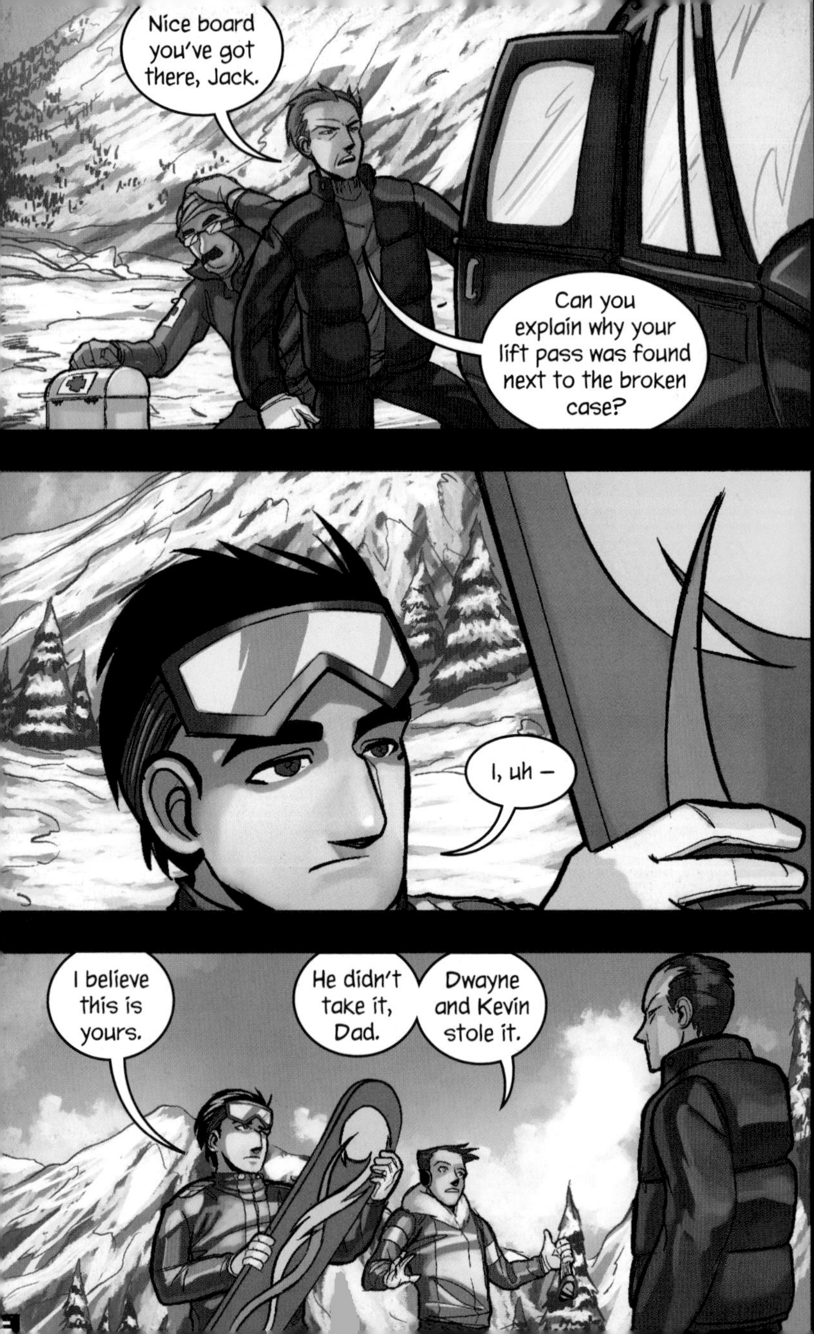
Nice board you've got there, Jack.
Can you explain why your lift pass was found next to the broken case?
I, uh –
I believe this is yours.
He didn't take it, Dad.
Dwayne and Kevin stole it.

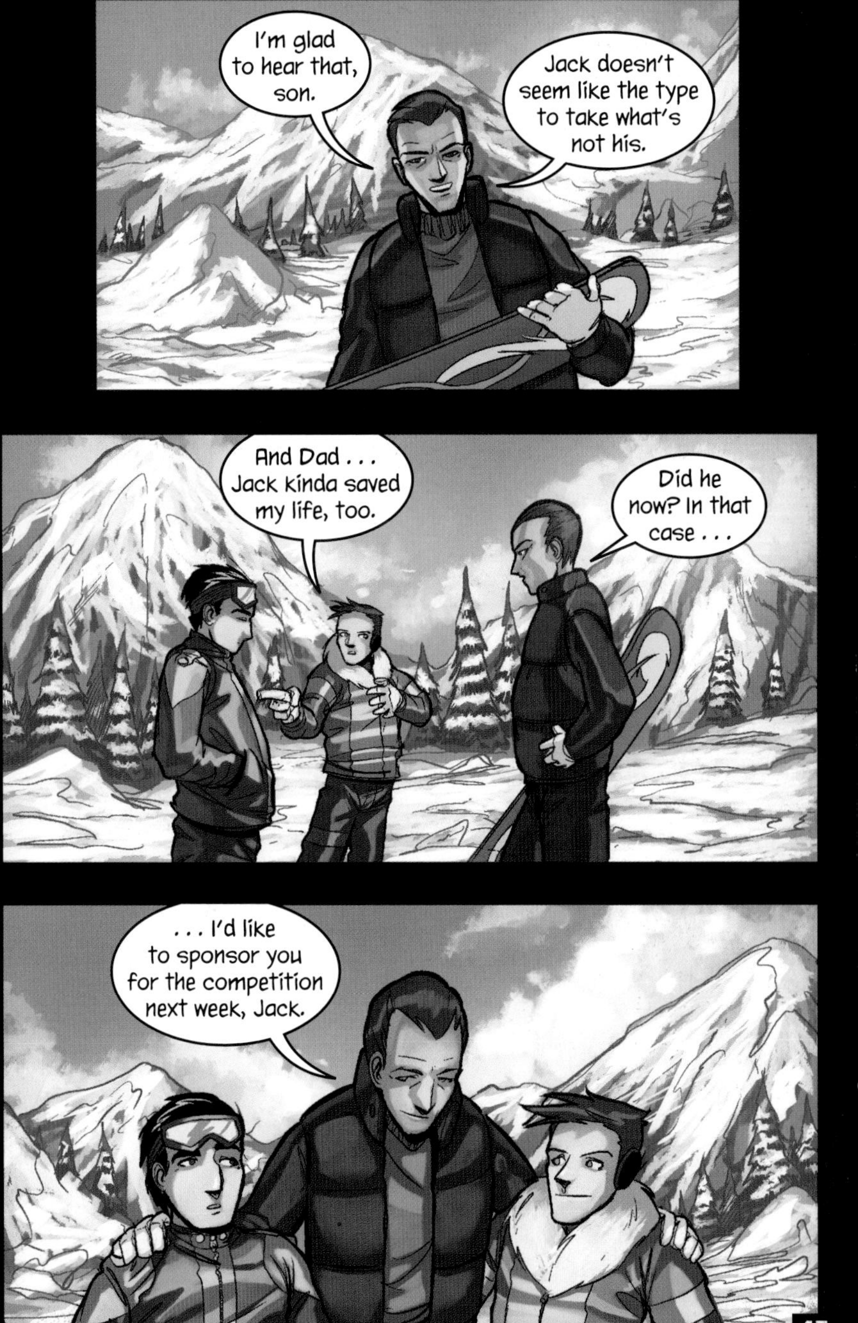
I'm glad to hear that, son.
Jack doesn't seem like the type to take what's not his.
And Dad . . . Jack kinda saved my life, too.
Did he now? In that case . . .
. . . I'd like to sponsor you for the competition next week, Jack.

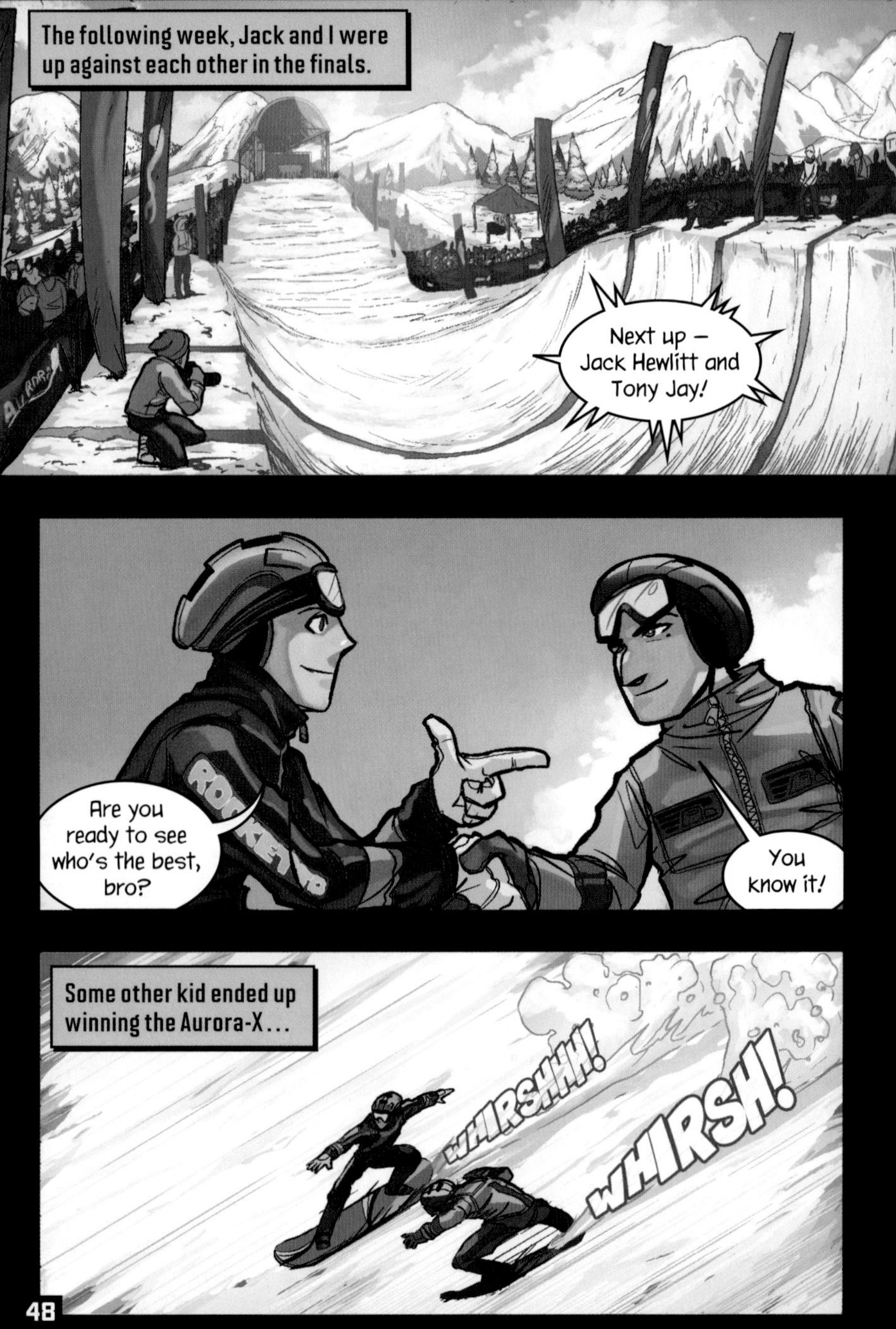

The following week, Jack and I were up against each other in the finals.
Next up — Jack Hewlitt and Tony Jay!
Are you ready to see who's the best, bro?
You know it!
Some other kid ended up winning the Aurora-X . . .
WHIRSHHH!
WHIRSH!

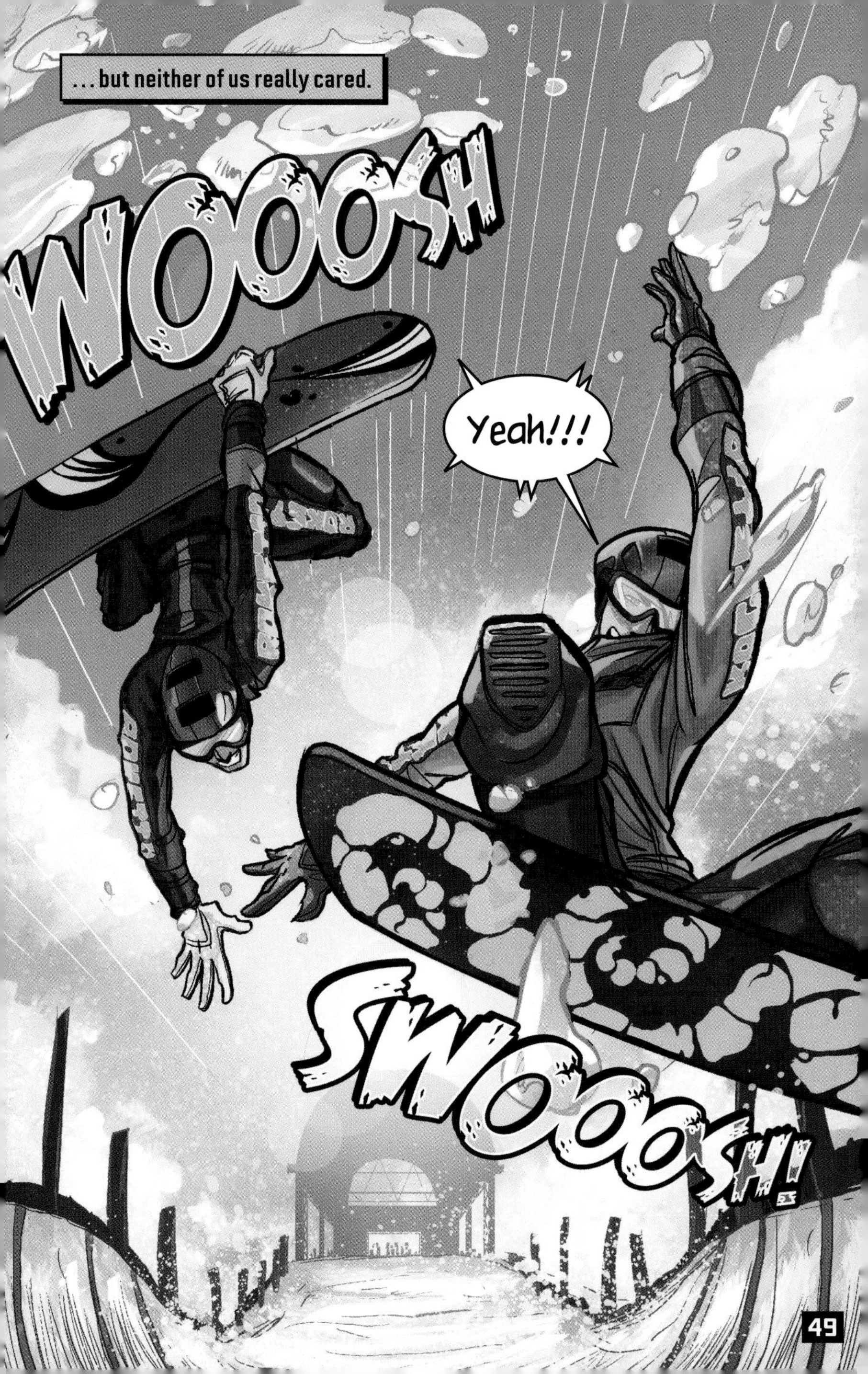

... but neither of us really cared.
WOOOSH
Yeah!!!
SWOOOSH!

PORTS ZONE

STGAME RECAP

0
OING

BITTER RIVALS BECOME FAST FRIENDS AFTER OUTRUNNING AVALANCHE TOGETHER

' THE IMBERS

'ESTYLE EVENT AL SCORES:

IY JAY: 9.6
:K HEWLITT: 9.6
TAGGART: 9.7

STORY: An avalanche interrupted a freestyle duel between Jack Hewlitt and Tony Jay this weekend. The two teens were competing for the Aurora-X under the assumption that Tony Jay would later win it in the tournament. The unexpected event didn't faze the two teens — they simply shredded their way down the mountain with the deadly maelstrom of snow and ice nipping at their bindings.

Sports Illustrated KIDS

UP NEXT: SI KIDS INFO CENTER

SZ POSTGAME EXTRA

WHERE **YOU** ANALYZE THE GAME!

BLZ vs BRS
3-1
TGR vs RDR
33-32
EAG vs BAN
14-7
SPA vs WLD
4-3
BAN vs WLD
21-15
RZR vs LIG
4-3
BLZ vs BRS
3-1

Snowboarding fans got a real treat today when Tony Jay faced off against Jack Hewlitt in the Silver Falls Freestyle Tournament. Let's go into the stands and ask some fans for their opinions on the day's events ...

DISCUSSION QUESTION 1

Tony Jay and Jack Hewlitt are total opposites in some ways. Do you think people who are very different can become good friends? Why or why not?

DISCUSSION QUESTION 2

Who do you like better — Tony Jay or Jack Hewlitt? What kinds of things do you like, and dislike, about each teen? Discuss your answers.

WRITING PROMPT 1

Imagine that you've won a snowboarding tournament, and your reward is a custom board! Name your new board, and write a few paragraphs about it. Then, draw a picture of your personalized reward.

WRITING PROMPT 2

Both Tony and Jack act like heroes at certain points in this book. Have you ever seen or done something heroic? What happened? Write about it.

(AIR)—if you grab air, you perform a jump of some sort

(AV-uh-lanch)—a large mass of snow, ice, and earth that suddenly moves down the side of a mountain

(BINDE-ingz)—the part of a snowboard that you connect boots to

(free-STILE)—a style of skiing or snowboarding focused on doing tricks

(HAF-pipe)—a U-shaped trench with smooth walls that is used by snowboarders for aerial tricks

(SHRED-ur)—a snowboarder, particularly a talented one

(SPON-sur)—to give money and support to someone who is competing in a contest of some kind

(SOO-pur-pipe)—a larger version of a regular halfpipe. The walls in a superpipe can measure as high as 20 feet.

CREATORS

SCOTT CIENCIN › Author

Scott Ciencin is a *New York Times* bestselling author of children's and adult fiction. He has written comic books, trading cards, video games, television shows, as well as many non-fiction projects. He lives in Sarasota, Florida with his beloved wife, Denise, and his best buddy, Bear, a golden retriever. He loves writing books for Stone Arch, and is working hard on many more that are still to come.

ABURTOV › Illustrator

Aburtov is a graphic designer and illustrator who has worked in the comic book industry for more than 11 years. In that time, Aburtov has colored popular characters like Wolverine, Iron Man, Punisher, and Blade. He recently created his own studio called Graphikslava. Aburtov lives with his beloved wife in Monterrey, Mexico, where he enjoys spending time with family and friends.

ANDRES ESPARZA › Inker

Andres Esparza has been a graphic designer, colorist, and illustrator for many different companies and agencies. Andres now works as a full-time artist for Graphikslava studio in Monterrey, Mexico. In his spare time, Andres loves to play basketball, hang out with family and friends, and listen to good music.

FARES MAESE › Colorist

Fares Maese is a graphic designer and illustrator. He has worked as a colorist for Marvel Comics, and as a concept artist for the card and role-playing games Pathfinder and Warhammer. Fares loves spending time playing video games with his Graphikslava comrades, and he's an awesome drum player.

Sports Illustrated KIDS GRAPHIC NOVELS

QUICK COMIC

TY TAGGART and EDWIN PEREZ in:

SKATEBOARD BREAKDOWN

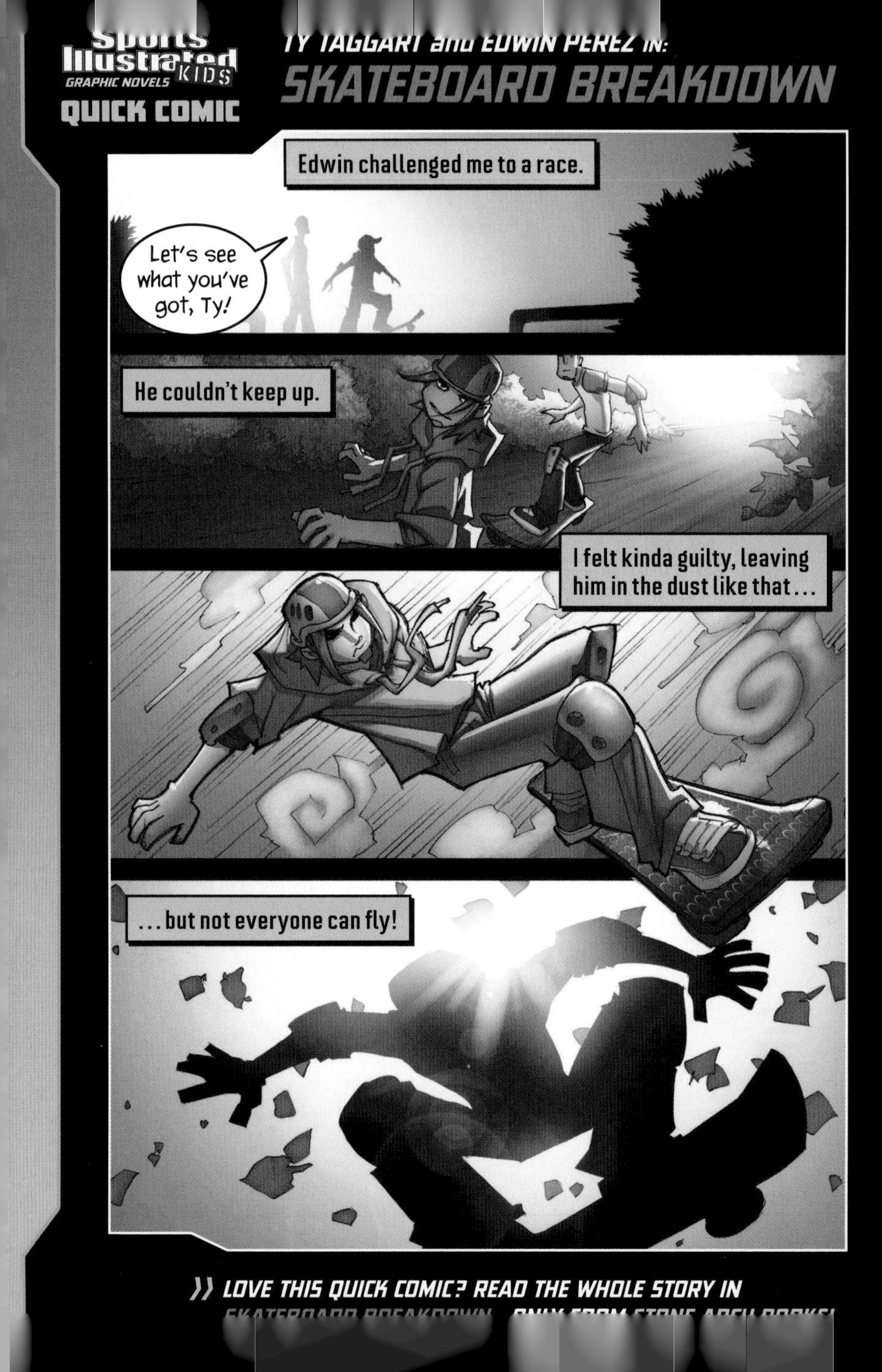
Edwin challenged me to a race.
Let's see what you've got, Ty!
He couldn't keep up.
I felt kinda guilty, leaving him in the dust like that . . .
. . . but not everyone can fly!

›› LOVE THIS QUICK COMIC? READ THE WHOLE STORY IN SKATEBOARD BREAKDOWN -- ONLY FROM STONE ARCH BOOKS!

HOT SPORTS.
HOT FORMAT!

GREAT CHARACTERS BATTLE FOR
SPORTS GLORY IN TODAY'S HOTTEST
FORMAT—GRAPHIC NOVELS!

ONLY FROM STONE ARCH BOOKS

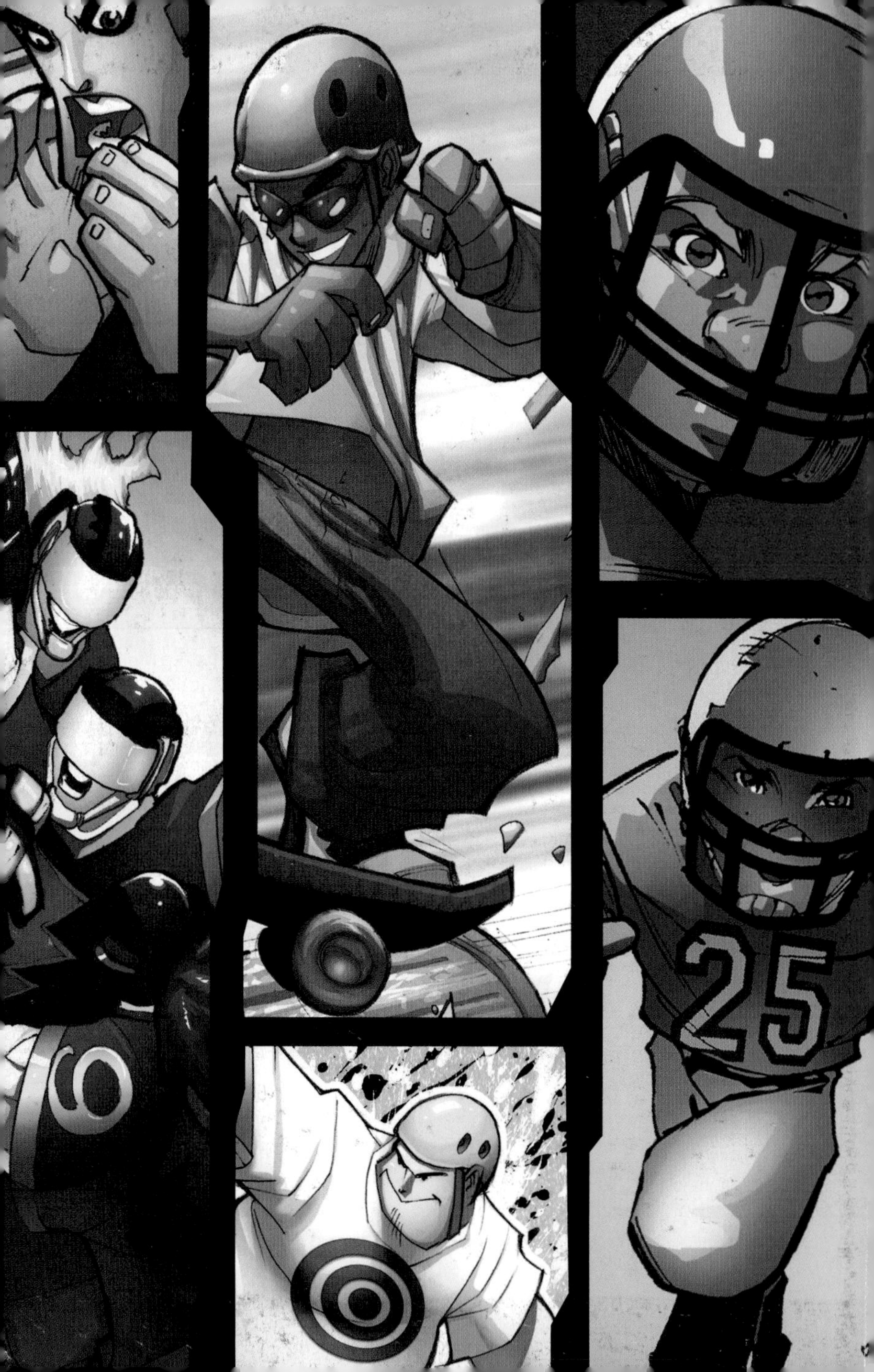